Snapdragons

KITTY FITZGERALD, born in Ireland, was raised in Scawthorpe, Doncaster. Her father was a Bridsworth Colliery miner, her mother a mill worker in Bradford. On her marriage she moved to Norton, then to Devon and Newcastle upon Tyne, where at the age of thirty she began writing. She is the author of a ground-breaking novel *Marge* (Sheba 1984), a collection of short stories called *Tight Corners*, and two plays, *Can't See the Wood for the Trees* and *Break My Bones*. She has written drama for film and for BBC Radio 4, and her film *Dream On* was awarded the most original screenplay at Le Baule Festival of European Films, the Prix de Public at the International Festival in Cretil, and the Northern Electric Arts Award for Authorship.

Snapdragons
Kitty Fitzgerald

BRANDON

A Brandon Original Paperback

Published in 1999 by
Brandon
an imprint of Mount Eagle Publications Ltd
Dingle, Co. Kerry, Ireland

ISBN 0 86322 258 7

(original paperback)

10 9 8 7 6 5 4 3 2 1

This book is published with the assistance of
the Arts Council / An Chomhairle Ealaíonn

Cover design by Public Communications Centre, Dublin
Typeset by id communications, Tralee
Printed by The Guernsey Press Ltd, Channel Islands

For Dan and Jack

— ONE —

THERE WAS ONLY a year between me and my sister Deirdre, but that sliver of maturity meant I had all the lousy jobs to do: fetch the water, feed the bad-tempered goat, clean out the hen house, bring the peat indoors and run the gauntlet of that filthy old sod, Gerald, who ran the creamery. He had hands to spare. Some said he was the illegitimate son of Tommy Reilly, who trained horses and owned the big house at Mulcahey's bend, apparently bred of a secret liaison between him and the priest's housekeeper, Molly Cahill. Some said. Anyway, he got the creamery business from somewhere and he was a menace to boys and girls alike.

One winter's day Deirdre had to go to the creamery for the milk and butter because I was laid up with measles. I'll hand it to her, Deirdre doesn't hold back. She came screaming out of Gerald's office and straight into the church, where mass was in progress. Up on to the altar she flew and threw herself at the feet of Father Molloy.

"Burn him in hell!" she screamed, over and over again, until Molly Cahill had the sense to slap her and pour holy water over her head. It did the trick right enough, but no one knows to this day if it was the slap or the water that silenced Deirdre. Gerald became the focus of Father Molloy's "intentions" for the next month. It seems his soul was saved because he never laid a finger on any of us again, though the rumour was that a surgeon friend of Tommy Reilly's had been employed to do a bit of pertinent snipping. Personally, I think the sound of Deirdre screeching on the altar had a lot to do with it. Certainly scared the shit out of everyone else.

There was no denying Deirdre's beauty. She had the pale-skinned, dark-haired delicacy of a holy icon, with the promise of leashed-up passion fizzing behind her eyes. Beneath the skin was chaos, something unresolved. My earliest encounter with her demons took place when I was eight. We shared the same bed, top to tail. I woke in the pitch blackness of a Sunday morning with my head on fire. Deirdre had placed the point of a darning needle on my scalp and was holding a lit candle to the centre of it. Hot wax sizzled.

"Just wanted t'see what happened," she said when I yelled at her, so I slapped her and she cried and Dad belted me with the fire strap. Perhaps she was showing early scientific genius, curiosity, inventive zeal. She certainly got away with murder, literally.

My favourite hen, Ursula, was the victim. She pecked Deirdre's ankles once too often and got her neck squashed in the garden gate in retribution. There was no point telling Dad I saw her do it, saw the spark in her eyes as she lured Ursula to her death with juicy titbits. I was the cuckoo in the nest; at least, that's what it felt like.

Mam and Dad were distant with me, at arm's length, emotionally and physically. He worked our bit of land and helped out when Johnny McGuire needed extra hands for his building projects or Tommy Reilly was harvesting and such like. Mam made ends meet, fed and watered us, kept the house ticking over. If Deirdre was a goddess then I was the gargoyle on her temple. I was short where she was tall, plump where she was slim. My voice rasped like a tractor engine; hers had the tone of an expensive harp. What with my parents' indifference, Deirdre's nastiness and God constantly on my case, it's a marvel that I developed any self-respect. God tried to tell me that it was His way of testing my faith, but, as these things tend to go, 'twas me ended up testing Him.

Nothing much could be kept secret in our village. The church was the focus of everything and Father Molloy was God's representative on earth. That was why he was one of the few people to own a car thereabouts. Molly Cahill was the fountain of gossip and not to be crossed lightly. Her sister, Kathleen, ran the store and filled in all the gaps in Molly's knowledge. We kids were watched by all the adults, a sort of communal parenting, so that it was hard to get away with any mischief.

Still, we had our network too, which informed us of misdemeanours committed behind closed doors and perhaps owned up to in the confessional. We had few illusions about our elders and, apart from Father Molloy, thought them a queer old bunch; especially old coots like Nat Dolan, who was fifteen going on seventy and much younger in head than body. Molly Cahill used to whisper about "a weakness" when discussing him, but we knew that incest was the term she was avoiding.

We had a village water pump around which hurling was a regular pastime, one store, the church overshadowing everything, and a row of four old terraced cottages housing farm workers. Our one-storey house was three miles up the valley; great if you were coming down by bike, torture going back. The school was in the middle of a field between the two places, with a shrine to the Blessed Virgin on the corner as you turned into the lane.

Unlike Gerald, Nat Dolan could be trusted not to molest, and so we let him pretend he was one of us when he turned up with his hurling stick or towel for swimming in the river. Me and Breda were also desperately curious as to whether his old dangly bit had ever been out to play, but these were thoughts we kept for dark nights of whispering when Deirdre was well out of earshot.

Nat Dolan's boss on Cashel's farm was called Timmon. He was a man of few words, most of them nasty, and terrible contrary into the bargain. He employed local labour on a casual basis for things like potato picking, mostly schoolkids. We were grateful for the pittance he paid, though most of it went to our mams. Deirdre insisted on coming with us one day when we went on one of our illicit forays to liberate spuds from Timmon's fields. Our intention was to cycle with them to the next village and sell them. Well, he'd have stolen the eye out of your head if you'd let him. There was me, Breda, Niall, Mick and Deirdre. I knew Deirdre had only come because she had a fancy for Mick. He was fourteen and the oldest of the bunch.

While we struggled to fill the sacks Deirdre kept a lookout, being too delicate to heave spuds. Typically, she spent more time watching Mick than keeping an eye out for Timmon. Breda saw him hurtling over the hill towards us brandishing a shotgun. We ran, of course, but he'd been cuter than us. The Gardaí were waiting at the end of the lane, their battered black car askew on the road. They rounded us up like cattle. It was then that I noticed Deirdre was missing.

Back at home, knowing the Gardaí would be calling at the house later, I stared at Deirdre. She was standing by the fire brushing Grandma May's hair, pretending I didn't exist. I willed all sorts of ills on her. It was hours before I caught her alone, in the peat shed.

"Well?" I asked angrily.

"He was very kind," she said peevishly. "I showed him the sty that was coming on my eye and he told me to go home and stay away from you lot."

"You cried, didn't you?" I said disgustedly.

"I couldn't help it. My sty was hurting," she answered triumphantly, secure in the knowledge that, once again, she'd escaped punishment. That night, after the Gardaí had called, I was given a thrashing by Grandma May. I had welts the size of large worms all over my legs, which I displayed angrily to Deirdre in our attic bedroom. She ignored me completely and, when I'd finished threatening her, got down on her knees by the bed and prayed for my soul to be saved from eternal damnation. She made sure her voice was loud enough for Mam and Dad to catch every word. I dreamt of the Day of Judgement and pictured myself hauled up before St Peter carrying a sack of potatoes. Deirdre was sitting on the right side of God, who as usual bore a remarkable resemblance to Father Molloy.

The tinkers came during the summer of my sixteenth birthday. Their camp was in a field by the river which ran behind the church. The inevitable warnings were given about steering clear of them, about what holy terrors they all were. It didn't stop groups of us watching them from a safe distance, fascinated by their carry-on. They knew things we didn't, I was sure of that. One lad of about my own age caught my eye particularly. When he left the camp and came up the lane towards the spot where me and Breda were hiding, I felt my insides leaping.

"Come on out," he said as he stopped by the ditch. "I won't bite you."

He was skinny like a twig but desperately gorgeous with his crow-black hair, chocolate eyes and welcoming mouth. There was mischief written on every line of his face. He was called Jake, and the more I saw of him the more I became aware of parts of my body that had never troubled me before. I was fierce with a passion for him. Mam thought I had a fever and tried to keep me indoors. A fruitless exercise.

He met me from my work at the schoolmaster's house most evenings. I felt ashamed of my red, dry hands and crumpled work clothes, but as soon as he touched my arm I forgot everything. We kissed, lay together, he nuzzled my breasts, tickled my thighs. I trembled and sighed and waited for the moment when he would finally go all the way. He said that he'd learned that anticipation added to the thrill. I told Breda everything and we screeched and laughed till our ribs hurt.

Of course I'd put up with lots of fumblings over the years from lads round and about and from the frantic mad auld fellas who lunged at you like a hungry man's fork at a sausage at every opportunity. Sometimes I'd had to fight like a rabid dog, but I must have had a guardian angel of sorts because most of my friends had been "had",

one way or another, before they reached sixteen. Breda
and I looked out for each other. Besides which we were
terrified of the wrath of God and his representative on
earth, Father Molloy. Most of all I was stopped by the
certain condemnation and abandonment which would
be forthcoming from my parents, who seemed to like me
little enough as it was. Perhaps I wanted to prove something
to them. Even so, when they tried to marry me at sixteen
to that red-haired, sixty-year-old farmer from west Cork,
I dug my heels in and reinforced their disapproval of me.
He had a big square face, a splash of red hair and hands
the size of a sow's head. When I saw those hands I felt my
stomach turn like bad milk at the thought of them at me
night after night.

There was dancing on the last night of the tinkers'
stay and I was determined to go and at last give up my
virginity to Jake. Breda conspired with me and invited me
to stay at her house which was on the far side of the river.
Her parents were both deaf, so it was easy to sneak out.
As I packed a bundle to take with me, Deirdre sauntered
into the bedroom.

"Don't think I don't know what you're up to," she said.
"Half the village is talking about your carrying-on with
that lad."

"So?" I replied.

"So, you'll take me with you to Breda's or else I'll tell
Grandma May what's going on."

I didn't argue. Deirdre's threats were never idle, and
besides I was too excited for even her to upset me. I should
have known better. I saw Jake look Deirdre up and down
when we arrived at the camp and my anticipation curdled.

I wanted to throw myself at his feet and shout "No! No! Not her!", but Breda stopped me from making an entire fool of myself. Deirdre giggled and crooned over him the whole evening. From time to time he'd glance over at me and shrug his shoulders as if to say, "What can I do?" Meanwhile I seethed and Breda sympathised. When they disappeared into the bushes, Breda and I gave up and headed back to her house, but we couldn't sleep. Instead we went through our list of swear words and shouted them out into the night sky. Deirdre crept in at two in the morning. Her face glowed beneath her tangled hair. I turned my back on her and bit my lip till it bled.

I couldn't understand why Jake hadn't taken me earlier. I'd been all too willing. I should have been bolder, I told myself. Nine months later I was glad I hadn't as I helped Deirdre through a difficult and painful delivery. The baby only lived for two days. Grandma May died of a stroke a week later. I've never known for sure whether the two events were connected, but I spent a lot of time cursing God the Father, the Son and the Holy Ghost that week.

I'd never been too happy with the pale-faced, wavy-haired Jesus Christ who inhabited our church. He looked as if he had no fun at all in him. Breda and I were convinced he couldn't ever have experienced the stirrings of sexuality, otherwise his eyes would have sparkled more. Still, that could have been the fault of the sculptor, but the Christ who let Deirdre get pregnant and then took the baby and Grandma May away from her was a cruel old devil, that's for sure. That was when I began to wonder if the Holy Trinity existed just so that They could blame each other for inadequacies and inconsistencies.

That was the fault of the Holy Ghost; or Jesus did that; or God the Father looks after that area. They didn't fool me. I lumped Them all into the one package: God – not to be trusted.

Grandma Isobel, who lived at Ardfinnan, saw me deliberately chewing the Host after communion one Sunday. A top-grade mortal sin, alongside buggery, in the scheme of things. She took me for a stroll in the graveyard after mass and locked on to me with her soft, pea-green eyes.

"Why are you so cross with God, Bernadette?" she enquired.

"He's cruel. He hurts people. How can he be the God of love?"

"It's not our place to know the extent of His plan. What looks to us like a meanness here and there may have significant good effects in the long run. You have to learn trust, learn to rely on the inherent goodness of Him."

What could I say to that? Isobel was the most generous of women, the one I would always run to if I had trouble. And I knew, if anyone loved me, it was her.

"Will you try?" she asked. I nodded. "Talk to Him. Question Him. He's always listening and sometimes He replies." I nodded again, and with that she took me to her house for boiled bacon sandwiches and rhubarb pie. As I ate she read to me from the bible. And that's one of the lasting things about Irish Catholicism: you discover that there's misfortune waiting at the end of every rainbow, and, if there isn't, you'll create it right enough.

Isobel sent me home with a quote from Ecclesiasticus to ponder: "It is a foolish thing to make a long prologue and to be short in the story itself." I took it to mean I should get a grip on life and stop fiddling about in the question department. And, as I walked up Kilsha in the dusky light, God did indeed speak to me. His voice seemed to emanate from a big border of fragrant snap-dragons in front of Ormond's farm. He told me I was a right little eejit.

— TWO —

DEIRDRE TOOK SOME time to recover. I watched over her, my jealousies overcome by less selfish feelings. Once she was back on her feet I retreated into envy. She couldn't do heavy work because the birth had taken its toll on her "insides", as Mam chose to call them. It meant more graft for me and less time to myself, and I had little enough of that as it was. When it came to dances in neighbouring villages, Deirdre had to have the bike and I had to walk. I was filled with a sense of injustice. She was no nicer than she'd ever been.

I'd always had the idea that she was more than a bit demented. When she started setting her sights on a distant cousin of ours, Billy Conlin, the MC at most of the local dances, I felt justified in my suspicions. He was fat, balding and a constant teller of boring jokes. Even his mother, Aunt Noleen, strong Catholic that she was, raised her eyes to heaven when he started on.

Aunt Noleen had buried three husbands. The first had been Billy's dad, the second a half-brother of my mam's and the third a widower thirty years her senior. It was common gossip that she'd bumped them all off with a combination of over-mothering and a rasping voice which never seemed to tire of spouting inanities. Chinese water torture had nothing on Noleen.

I could see why Billy might fancy Deirdre, but her

apparent attraction to him was a mystery, until we found out that his future plans included living in England. Deirdre had fancied that particular trip for long enough.

I think Billy Conlin was as surprised as everyone else when Deirdre accepted his fumbling proposal of marriage. Mam gritted her teeth. She'd expected better things of Deirdre; Billy Conlin would have done for me. Yes, she said that. Still, she folded her arms, did her sums and the plans were made. Six months later the ceremony took place. I will admit that Deirdre looked gorgeous. Next to her Billy seemed more pathetic than usual, but his face shone with some inner light of expectation. I don't think he got what he expected, but by the end of the day I was too drunk to care and found myself in the peat shed with Mick.

He had no more real experience in sexual matters than me. I think we were just going through the motions, encouraged by too much drink. I liked Mick. He was gentler than most of his pals, a joker, a bit of a dreamer. We gave up the pretence of doing anything after a while, preferring to sit and talk about what a weird old deal Billy Conlin was getting and other interesting stuff.

Mick had an uncle up in Dublin who was wild into politics. He sent down newspaper cuttings, leaflets, handouts, seeing it as his duty to "spread word of the struggle". Without his regular missives we'd have had little or no idea what was going on. Not that we had great understanding as it was.

"He's raving on about the IRA campaign in the North at the minute," Mick said. "He calls them 'fine boys' and reckons the Six Counties policy is in terminal decline.

'The house of cards is tumbling,' he says."

"What's your idea?" I asked.

"What do I know?" he said. "I hear the auld fellas in the bar rooting on about it all, and they seem to be caught up in the past and blinded by religion."

"Jesus, Mick," I laughed, "don't let Father Molloy hear you say that or you'll be publicly condemned at mass."

When we eventually ambled back into the party, looking a bit dishevelled and smelling of peat, Mam got hold of me by the ear and pinned me up against the pantry door.

"You little eejit," she hissed. "You've got little enough to offer, at least you could save it for the proper time."

That was the full extent of my sex education, and a good example of Mam's attitude towards me. I always seemed to create pain rather than pleasure for her, no matter how hard I tried. Sometimes, she looked at me with eyes so remote I felt she was observing a stranger. Dad was merely indifferent. If it hadn't been for Deirdre I might have thought parents were just like that, but she was treated like a precious object. A situation she capitalised on at every turn.

I'd toyed with the idea that I was adopted, but I looked so much like Grandma Isobel I knew it was just a fantasy. My early plans had been to journey off and find my "real" parents, who would be pleased to see me, be very wealthy and love me properly. When I could no longer entertain that scenario, I would look around the village and feel a terrible barrier between me and the rest of the world. Then I would go to Isobel's and get her to tell me tales about Grandad Joseph and the Irish Republican Brotherhood and Michael Collins and Grainne O'Malley, and I'd feel refreshed and part of something.

God always seemed to talk to me after a visit to
Isobel's, but I didn't much like what He had to say: "The
imagination of man's heart is evil from his youth," for
example, and "I am a jealous God visiting the iniquities
of the fathers on the children." Sometimes He just
laughed, long and loud. Other times He whispered in
Latin, phrases from mass and other things I didn't understand. I frequently told Him to go to hell, and He'd
respond with something odd and yet close to the mark,
like, "Can a man take fire in his bosom, and his clothes
not be burned?" Sometimes I wondered if I wasn't a
penny short of a shilling myself.

I watched for signs of growth in Deirdre's belly and so
it seems did everyone else. There was scandalous gossip
about whether she was using some form of contraceptive
contraption. Mam deflected it all with odd phrases about
Deirdre's "insides". Billy Conlin bloomed less as the
months went by. Of course Mam had had her share of
comments to put up with in the past, only having two
children while all around her families were multiplying
by the score. Perhaps that was why she understood
Deirdre's "insides" so well. But I had the sneaking suspi-
cion that Deirdre was well in control of all her bodily
needs and Billy's baby wasn't included on the list.

I wasn't allowed to go to Dublin to see them off. Mam
said something about getting ideas above my station.
Little did she know. My plans were growing by the day.
I'd decided to take a leaf out of Deirdre's book, minus the
marriage. I nosed around for months trying to find a way
to get passage out of the place where I knew every brick

and blade of grass. I pumped people unmercifully for information, aware that Deirdre was not going to invite me over. In the end the answer was – as it usually is – right under my nose, or, to be precise, in my red, chapped hands.

The schoolmaster who I "did" for – Mr Cleary – was a widower whose bones were fast decaying and whose skills as a teacher had never developed. But he had managed to produce one offspring who'd left the fold before I began to walk. Mr Cleary hadn't ever visited England and he suddenly decided to go. A last-gasp trip. Best of all, he asked permission for me to accompany him and made Mam a monetary offer she obviously couldn't refuse. Besides which, I overheard Dad saying he'd be glad to see the back of me. Eavesdroppers never hear anything good of themselves, God sneered. I took no notice.

I was delirious with excitement. Breda was green with envy. I promised I'd find a way of getting her over to join me, because I had no intention of returning once the two weeks' holiday was over. I was following the advice of Ecclesiasticus. The prologue was over; it was time to move on to the main story.

I had few regrets about leaving the family nest. Only Grandma Isobel had given me the affection I craved. I saw it as a chance to leave God behind for good. He told me in no uncertain terms that I would regret following the lures of Satan. He wasn't laughing at the time.

Mr Cleary had booked us a double cabin on the boat and in the middle of the night attempted to put his half-erect penis inside me. My screams brought a steward running, by which time I'd nearly battered the old man to death with his walking stick. The steward took me off and made me sweet tea and sickly propositions of his own. I spent the rest of the trip in the women's lavatory, which reeked of gin and vomit.

When the boat finally docked in Liverpool, I crept back to the cabin to collect my belongings, sparse as they were. Mr Cleary was dressed and polished.

"Ah, there you are, Bernadette. I wondered where you'd got to," he said briskly. "Do hurry, my dear, or we'll be last to get off."

It wasn't my first taste of hypocrisy, but it was a bold attempt.

— THREE —

MR CLEARY JUNIOR – Ted – was a miner working in the pits in Yorkshire. His wife, Joan, welcomed me with a newly-made bed, bacon and eggs, and a laugh that would wake the dead.

They lived on a purpose-built National Coal Board estate, in one of about a hundred houses designed around a green area for recreation. Three bedrooms, two living rooms, a kitchen, bathroom and garden: it seemed like absolute luxury to me. A mansion. A place Tommy Reilly would have been proud of owning and Father Molloy would have visited regularly. People were in and out of one another's houses at the drop of a hat and there was a general air of optimism about the place. A sort of sense of knowing who you were and what you were doing. Certainly, behind closed doors there were as many problems as I'd experienced at home, but outwardly life seemed to be on the up and up.

Britain was rebuilding itself after World War II. Government commissions had brought workers from other countries to help in the reconstruction. Here they were, all thrown together: Irish, Italian, Polish, Yugoslav, stirred in with Scots, Welsh, Geordies and the original Yorkshire mixture. Volatile it was. It seemed that someone was always screaming and shouting, day and night, in and out of doors. Voices of operatic quality and strength sang, in umpteen languages, strange songs of other times, other places.

There seemed to be a future here, a place that was being aimed for, change, progress, new ideas. I felt optimistic and scared at the same time.

When Ted described his work at the colliery I could almost taste the dust on my tongue. My stomach lurched as he talked about the cage that took them from the surface to the coal-face. I tried to imagine what it felt like spending all those hours in darkness, often unable to stand up straight all day long. What did it feel like being so much closer to hell than the rest of us? I asked the question out loud without intending to and everyone laughed. Old man Cleary took the opportunity to wrap his seaweed arm around me and try to fondle my right breast. Joan must have seen what was happening because she stood on his corns and pulled me away, "to help her with the dishes".

I loved her instantly, right down to the roots of her peroxide hair. She felt so warm and approachable and seemed to like me without any difficulty. I felt safe with her. She wrapped chubby arms around me as I went to bed that first night and I blurted out my fears of a second visitation by old man Cleary. I heard her bellowing through the floorboards seconds after she'd left the room. Then she came back with a mug of cocoa and a copy of *Woman and Home* magazine.

"He'll not be trying owt tonight, duck," she said. "But, if it makes you feel better, shove the chest of drawers up against the door when I've gone." I did.

I'd never seen a woman's magazine before. One shilling

it cost, which seemed like a small fortune to me, as my
weekly wage from old Cleary was less than ten bob. The
front cover had a painting of a glamorous woman wearing
a white hat and dress. She had matching earrings and
necklace in red and white, virtually no eyebrows and
bright red lips. I thought she looked very sophisticated.
There were knitting patterns for a "Batwing in Bouclé"
and a "Lacy Jersey in 2-ply". The advertisements told me
that Britain's up-and-coming girls use Silvikrin shampoo;
that Puritan soap keeps hands smooth and lovely; that
fair hair is always in fashion with Hiltone; and that
Gibbs SR toothpaste keeps teeth white and gums bright.
I looked at myself in the mirror and realised what a
hayseed I looked.

The thing that really caught my attention was the "new
romantic serial" by Sara Seale. It was called "The Dark
Stranger". Next to the illustration of a man and woman
gazing off into the distance, it said: "There are few situations more touching than that of a young girl who has
never been shown real tenderness." That was it. I started
sobbing at once. I felt very sorry for myself, unloved,
alone and frightened in this new place. At that instant
I realised I even missed Father Molloy. I attempted to
communicate with God, but He wasn't listening or else
He was playing hard to get. I went back to the magazine
and fell asleep reading the Problem Page: "I am worried
about my daughter because she always seems so
discontented . . . "

Next day Ted took his father off sightseeing and Joan
took me under her wing. I learnt more about her in a
day than I've learnt about other people in twenty years,

especially when she confided in me about her affair with
a deputy at the pit.

"Ted would go spare," she said, "but I've done him a
lot of good. Got him on a good team earning better
money. Jack, my man, he sees to things like that, you
know. It started off all innocent like, just the odd hello
down the bookie's, then before I knew what was what we
were at it like bloody rabbits. It's passion, duck. You're
too young to understand now, but there's a vast difference
between love and passion. For a start, one lasts and the
other doesn't, unless it's on the side like me and Jack, 'cos
that gives it an added thrill, you know."

I didn't know then. But I thought I might learn a thing
or two from Joan if I stuck around. She took me into
the town centre and nearly laughed herself silly when I
picked up a wire basket outside a supermarket.

"But it says 'Please take one'," I spluttered as a shop
assistant ran after me.

"Only for shopping in the store," Joan laughed. "Eeh,
what are you like."

I rode on a double-decker bus and found it hard to
believe we weren't going to end up flying, we seemed so
high up. In one of the clothes shops a woman mistook my
accent for Polish. "Bloody foreigners," I heard her say
under her breath.

"Tek no notice, duck," Joan said loudly. "That's the
trouble with posh folk; they haven't got any manners."

Sitting in a small teashop near the market-place, I
drank my first cup of coffee.

"Like it?" Joan asked.

"Not sure."

"Ooh, I love it. Perhaps it'll grow on yer. I feel like a film star when I drink it."

We went to see Mario Lanza and Ann Blyth at the Picture House in *The Great Caruso*. We cried and laughed and I longed for Breda to be there with me, sharing all the new experiences. Travelling back to her house later, Joan gave me her potted philosophy on life: "There's a lot of ignorance around, Bernie – prejudice and downright stupidity. Don't let it trouble you too much. In the south they think everybody with a northern accent is thick. In the north they have their own scapegoats, the foreigners. It's a rum old world if you take it too seriously."

She reminded me of Isobel, and it felt so good to be liked I could have stayed and stayed. Unfortunately, her Ted had wandering hands like his dad. I couldn't face telling Joan so I skipped off, pinching a fiver from old man Cleary's pocket in the process. He owed me more than he'd ever pay back.

Deirdre and Billy were in Birmingham, so that's where I headed. The bus travelled through miles and miles of built-up area with smoke churning out of countless chimneys and barely a patch of green to be seen. When we pulled into the terminus I just wanted to wish myself back to Joan's, even back home and take the consequences. It was all so alien and hostile. Too much noise; too many people; strange metallic smells. It was as if an architect had gone mad while drawing up the plans but everyone had taken him seriously. I wondered how anyone could live in the place and maintain any degree of sanity.

I'd only a few pennies left by the time I located the address Deirdre had sent home. It was a ground-floor flat in Sparkbrook. I rang the bell three times before getting a reply. Billy looked awful. Red-rimmed eyes, belly out of control, unshaven. He didn't recognise me at first.

"What?" he said. "Not the bloody Jehovas again."

"It's me, Billy. Bernadette."

"Oh God." He stepped back. "Come on, come in." As I followed him down the hall of many colours he stopped and gave me a cold eye. "Has she sent you?" he asked.

"Who?"

"Deirdre, of course!"

"Isn't she here?"

"Is she hell as like! Anyway, come in; tell me when you arrived. You'll take a spot of tea, won't you?"

I stopped then, reluctant to enter another lion's den, yet desperate for somewhere to stay. There was some spark still left in him because he recognised my hesitation for what it was.

"Jesus," he sighed. "I've had enough on with that sister of yours. I've no intention of laying hands on you, don't you worry."

So there I was. Well, Michael Collins had survived ten years in England and returned to Ireland a more determined man. And look what happened to him, God said, ever cheerful.

An unlikely combination turned into a useful partner-ship. Billy was quite incapable of looking after himself. I blame his mother; she never even taught him to boil an egg.

He encouraged me to speak more slowly so that I could make myself understood. He showed me the local shops, the bus stops, and introduced me to Sha, who came round the street each week selling goods out of the back of an old van and gave credit after you'd been a good customer for a while. But he said very little about Deirdre, just had this haunted look in his eyes and jumped with anticipation every time the doorbell rang, yet seemed reluctant to answer it. Like he was waiting for good news and bad news all rolled into one. He lived on tinned soup, pilchard and tomato sauce sandwiches, and the weakest tea that I ever saw. Every now and then he'd talk about "home" and get big lollopy tears in his eyes as if it had been heaven on earth.

"If it's so good, my man, then why have you never been back for a visit or two, eh?" I asked him.

"Oh I will, I will. I'll be going back when I've enough made. Believe me."

It was a phrase I was going to become very familiar with over the years to come. Slowly does it, like an ass to a thistle.

I set to and cleaned the place up, did some shopping, bought some clothes from a second-hand shop, and discovered that not everybody liked the Irish but they thought that the "coloureds" were worse. I was learning fast.

Billy was working as a barman at a city-centre pub frequented mostly by exiles like himself. He got me a part-time job cleaning and making doorstep sandwiches for the regulars. I knew how to clean and making sandwiches was no hard task, but I felt very much the child out of her depth and kept out of the way as much as possible. I told myself I'd get used to it before long.

There was often a sad sort of atmosphere in the pub, not easily detectable by outsiders. A sense of loss. But the loss of something not really understood, not completely

come to terms with. Towards the end of an evening
enough would have been drunk to drown a few sorrows.
Loud laughter and loud voices would disguise the lack of
ease. Arguments reared up frequently, but, the minute
someone began singing "Danny Boy" or "The Wild
Colonial Boy" or some such heart tugger, the wildest of
the bunch would turn his soft underbelly upwards in
surrender. They felt things they couldn't explain even to
themselves. They lashed out at each other, at strangers.
They stuck together. They were drawn to the past, living
for the future.

I wrote letters to Joan and Breda and anyone else at
home who I thought might be remotely interested. Joan
wrote back almost immediately:

> Dear Bernie,
> So glad you are safe. I was having kittens I can
> tell you, wondering if you were all right or in the
> clutches of another octopus. I got it out of Ted
> what he'd done. It was the last straw for me. I
> couldn't send him packing because the house was
> in his name, so I moved out. I'm up in a place
> called Highlands in digs with a Mr and Mrs
> Charlton. They're both seventy-odd and I get a
> cheap room in exchange for helping out. So, listen
> love, if you get stuck or need help write to me. If
> it's an emergency Jack's phone number at the pit is
> 573412, Jack Dickson. I mean it, Bernie.
> Love, Joan.

Gradually I discovered that I was a match for most of

the pub clients. I gave as good as I got and developed a
tolerance for poor jokes and hearty slaps on the back.
Within three weeks I felt as if I'd aged several years, and
that little hub of fear lurking behind my belly button
began to recede. I was going to make it. I was on the way
to being my own person. As the crackling of thorns under
a pot, so is the laughter of a fool, God said.

The city still held terror for me, but Digbeth End where
the pub was situated was relatively quiet. I could get a
bus to work direct from Sparkbrook without touching
the city centre. That suited me fine. The journey itself was
an education, packed like a wasp's nest on to buses carrying every creed and colour imaginable. The sound of three
or four or more different languages flying backwards and
forwards. Passion, fury, indifference, humour and plain
nastiness all canned up together.

Dan Kavanagh, the landlord of the Bull, kept everything
ticking over nicely. He had a natural charisma and quick
wit. This, together with the fact that he was five foot
eleven, solid as a steel girder and didn't suffer fools
gladly, made the atmosphere fairly easygoing. I watched
him from a distance, intrigued but wary. After all he was
an old man of about fifty and his obvious sensuality both
attracted and repelled me. At the end of six weeks Billy
and I were getting on like old pals. I knew I'd been right
all those years before to wish for a brother to replace
Deirdre. I began to think I'd given God too bad a press
and was just getting Billy round to the idea of Breda
coming over to live with us when Deirdre turned up.

She was furious to find me there and told me to pack
up and clear off in language that made my gums ache.

Billy shouted at her at first, but when she turned the waterworks on he melted. The last I saw of them that night was him carrying her into the bedroom as she nibbled his left earlobe and shot me a look of hatred over his oblivious shoulder. I hadn't expected a welcoming embrace, but the level of her hostility left me agitated and baffled.

Next morning I went off to work as usual. Deirdre wasn't going to get rid of me that easily. Billy turned up at lunchtime glowing like a lightbulb. "She doesn't want you staying on," he said. "I'm sorry, Bernie, but she is my wife."

"And how many times has she run out on you before this?" I said. I was determined to put up a fight.

"That isn't important. She's back now and she's staying this time. You know Deirdre, she's just a bit highly strung."

I resisted saying how highly strung I thought she should be. Billy was totally besotted and there's no reasoning with that illness. Dan Kavanagh saved the day. He had a small room vacant on the first floor of the pub. It was mine in exchange for extra hours. I wasn't spoilt for choice so I accepted. It would do temporarily. I wrote to Breda that afternoon, reassuring her of my continued endeavours to find a place for us both and filling in all the details of Deirdre and Billy's betrayal at great length.

Deirdre was still in bed when I got back to her place at four. The tea tray which Billy had obviously given her before leaving was littered with dog-ends. She had that bruised look that men find so attractive and I could see why Billy was enthralled. It didn't make me like her any the more; or him.

"I thought I told you to clear off," she rasped, her sweet voice now damaged by cigarettes and alcohol. "I didn't invite you here. I saw enough of you when we were growing up. Go and find someone else to scrounge off."

"Don't worry," I snarled. "I'm just collecting my things. I don't want to hang around here to watch you digging Billy's grave."

"He deserves everything he gets," she said. "He's as dull as ditchwater. You and he would make a good pair." She paused, assessing the level of my anger. I wouldn't give her the satisfaction of seeing how much she'd hurt me. "That's what you were angling for, wasn't it?" she continued. "A little love nest with Billy?"

"Don't be a fool," I snapped. "I've got better taste than that."

"Well, don't think I want you hanging around me cramping my style," she replied.

"What style?" I said, looking around pointedly. She got the point.

The fact that I was her sister seemed to have little or no significance to her. I wouldn't have turned her away if our roles had been reversed. Perhaps I was an unwelcome reminder of who she'd been and where she'd come from. Perhaps there was no way we could ever get on, too much done and said on both sides.

I left the room and shoved my few belongings into my bag.

"Please send any mail that comes for me to the pub," I said coldly as I made to leave.

"Does that include pleading letters from Mam?" she answered. "It'll break her heart to hear that you're skivvying at a pub."

"No it won't and well you know it," I replied. I could hear her laughter all the way down the street.

In my cold room that night I wrote to Mam and tried to explain what I was up to. Better that she hear it from me than get Deirdre's sordid version. I enclosed a note for Dad as well, although I was certain he would be completely indifferent. Mam, Dad and Deirdre, the unholy trinity that had no space for me.

Three in the morning found me talking to my absent God.

"If You are there then give me some sort of sign, something positive to show that You care," I pleaded.

A couple of hours later I was woken by a cold drip of water splashing on my face from the leaking roof. I pushed and pulled the heavy old bed to a new position away from the drip and stubbed my toe in the process. Thanks be to God! I hissed into the darkness. It was only the following day that I considered the possibility that Satan may have been on the loose. Or was that God's little let-out clause? Anything They don't like, blame on the devil.

— FOUR —

ON THE FRIDAY of the following week Billy came into work carrying a grubby envelope. He handed it to me with discomfort written all over his face. It had been opened and resealed.

"You're a fool, Billy," I said. "For God's sake, stop being a doormat to her and have a bit of bloody dignity."

"She opened it by accident, really," he said feebly. I managed to keep the tears under control until I was out of his sight. The letter was from Breda.

> Dearest Bernie,
>
> I was beginning to think I'd never get out of this hole and feeling jealous mad with envy about your new life over there. Now, it doesn't matter. Mick has asked me to marry him. Isn't that wonderful! I've always had a soft spot for him and he's working hard. So don't worry about me, I'm on the up and up. Keep in touch and you must come back for the wedding.
>
> Love, Breda

Plunk went my heart. So that was me, all alone in this place where the Irish and the coloureds were bottom of the dung- heap. I sobbed quietly until Dan banged on the door demanding that I set to on the lunchtime sandwiches.

It was awfully tempting to run back home there and then and forget all about living a life of my own. Only one small thing stopped me. I didn't have the fare.

The pub was crowded. Fridays always were. The long mahogany bar was lined with people starting their weekend early. I was like a headless chicken until two, when I stopped to drink some tea and leant on the end of the bar watching the proceedings. Billy called me into the back room, but I ignored him. Seconds later he came bustling in, flushed as a peach.

"There's a bloke from Waterford in the back, says he knows your family," he said.

It's part of being Irish. Wherever you go there's always someone who knows your family. I prepared myself for tales of how my mother was a living saint or how Grandad Joseph had been a true participant in the patriot game and so on.

I didn't recognise Jake at first. His hair was shorter and he was less tanned than when I'd last seen him, which was when he'd disappeared into the bushes with Deirdre all those years before.

I stared at him in disbelief for a second or two, until, unwilling to trust myself with words, I turned to walk away. His hand was on my arm in an instant. I wanted to die when I felt a thrill rush through my body. I shook him off and put distance between us. "I'll be in tonight, after nine," he said quietly. "Will I see you then?"

No reply is better than an incoherent babbling, so I left without a word. I carried the image of his face with me all afternoon and my arm tingled even after a scalding bath in the freezing bathroom. I called up memories of

Deirdre and the delivery to harden my attitude towards
him. It worked. A little. Billy came upstairs at nine-thirty
to tell me Jake was asking for me. His face was one big
question mark. Wouldn't he be stunned to hear the tale, I
thought vindictively.

We sat in the very back room where the only other
occupants were an elderly couple playing cards for half-
pennies. Awkward wasn't the word for it. Jake sat quietly,
leaving me to direct the pace of things. In the end curiosity
overcame me.

"How did you come to be here?" I asked.

He told me a long, rambling story about a fight with
his father and being banished from the camp accused of
becoming soft; of relatives in London where he'd first
stayed and of meeting a cousin in the building trade in
Birmingham. He was in digs in King's Heath.

"The posh end of the city, eh?" I remarked.

"Hardly. There's seven of us in the place. It resembles
a pigsty and I'm certain the pigs would complain at the
comparison."

"You left Deirdre in the shit," I said after minutes of
staring at the clock.

"I didn't know. I was oblivious."

"Would it have made any difference?"

"Who can say?"

"You bloody well can, you shite!"

The elderly couple gave me a long-suffering look. I
bared my teeth at them. I'd got the bull by the horns and
I wasn't letting go.

"She could have died like the baby and you not caring
tuppence. I wonder how many other girls have suffered a

similar fate at your hands."

He emptied the remains of his pint and indicated my half-empty glass. I shook my head.

"I never forced anybody in my life, so if that's what she told you she's lying."

I watched him at the bar. Lean and angular. His face deeply lined already, though he wasn't more than twenty-three. I hated myself for wanting him and I didn't understand how I could.

"Look," he said softly as he sat down again. "I was only a strip of a lad doing what lads do. I never thought beyond the next night. Why would I? We were long gone by the time she found she was pregnant, weren't we? How was I to know?"

The old couple left. Jake put his hand on top of mine. "It was you that really interested me," he said. "You must have realised that."

I couldn't trust myself with a response. I wanted what he said to be true so badly that my heart nearly stopped beating.

"You went with Deirdre," I said at last.

"Because it was the easy way out. There was something about you that frightened me, made me want to run and made me want to stay. I couldn't handle it, but I couldn't keep away. Why did you think I never made love to you?" I didn't have an answer. "So when Deirdre turned up . . . " he tailed off, looking down into his beer.

"But I've never been able to forget the way you looked at me that night. Do you hate me still?"

We made love in my cold attic room. I was transported back to the riverbank, the campfire, the music. I saw

Deirdre's look of disappointment as Jake left with me. The feeling of being wanted, of being selected over Deirdre, set me trembling. Jake was gentle, patient, his mouth was sweet, curious. I followed his lead until the demands of my own body made me daring and we shouted together into the darkness. Afterwards he sat up to smoke and gave me my first cigarette. Two firsts in one night. His face was sad but he pulled me close so that I couldn't look into his eyes.

"I've wanted to do that for nearly seven years," he said softly, "and now I desperately wish I hadn't."

I didn't have much time to react to this double-edged statement because a second later Deirdre burst into my room.

In the moment I had to consider it I thought I was going to get hell for sleeping with her former betrayer. How wrong can you be. I quickly discovered that there was nothing former about his betrayal. They'd been seeing each other for months. The times she'd left Billy, she'd been to Jake, only to return home after finding him with other women. It had occurred to me to wonder how he'd known about Deirdre's baby, but anger had driven the question from my mind. Now I knew. If I'd been disturbed at my own actions that night, I was even more appalled by Deirdre's. She clasped his head to her breast and stroked his hair continuously as tears gushed forth. I may as well have been invisible. She ignored me. Jake wouldn't look at me.

I left them to it. In the kitchen I made myself a pot of dark orange tea and stared at the floor. No one else stirred. When I went back to my room an hour later, Jake and Deirdre were in bed together fast asleep. All I could think was, at least he'd used a sheath. It tumbled around my head like a prayer.

Independent living suddenly felt a fearsome thing. Was there nothing in between the dull isolation and religious superstition of home and this grim experience I was living through? God help us, I hoped not.

God helps those who help themselves, came the reply, stating the obvious as usual.

— FIVE —

I THOUGHT AFTERWARDS that I should have woken the sleeping lovers, demanded my bed back and demanded an explanation for such desperate behaviour, but I was still a soft touch then. They looked like Hansel and Gretel escaping from a cruel world. I curled up on the lumpy armchair wrapped in a variety of coats and towels and eventually fell asleep to the rhythm of a thumping headache.

The bed was empty when I came to at nine in the morning, the bedclothes flung all over the floor. I looked down at the strangled sheets and recalled some of the sweetness that had come before the pain. I couldn't hold it for long. Dan Kavanagh interrupted me by bellowing up the stairs about where the hell was his ungrateful cleaner.

I set about work with gratitude. Displacement activity. Billy moved in and out of the bars and up and down to the cellar in silence. Once in a while he'd throw me a look of utter sadness. I don't know what I was expected to do. I'd told him over and over again that he should leave Deirdre. I certainly wasn't going to describe the events of the previous evening. So the web of deceit is woven.

"You think I'm stupid, don't you?" he blurted out over a cup of tea just before opening time. I said nothing, not trusting myself to be able to make any useful comment. "Love's a strange old thing, Bernie. One day you'll realise that." A huge sob escaped from his throat at this point. I patted his back until he recovered some composure.

"She's gone again," he said. I nodded. "She said she was never coming back this time."

"She's said that before, Billy. You told me. She threatens that every time she skips off. Anyway, what the hell, let her go."

Billy, poor, sad Billy, nearly broke my arm as he jumped up and pinned me against the bar door. I saw the monster inside the man for the first time.

"Don't ever talk about her as if she's rubbish," he said through grinding teeth.

He scared me. Physical violence does that. Dan saved the day by knocking us both flying as he pushed the door open to admit the first customers who'd been queuing outside. Billy and I avoided one another as well as we could. Then, about an hour before closing, he had to go down to the cellar. The minutes ticked by. Dan and I exchanged looks and he indicated for me to go and find Billy. I was tempted to refuse, but Dan was the boss.

I found him huddled in a corner behind some barrels. He was rocking and moaning and dribbling. What do you do in a situation like that? Especially when the bugger has recently tried to break your arm. I put myself in Grandma May's position. She never put up with blethering. I remember her dunking my head in a bucket of cow's milk once when I was crying about not getting a new frock for a dance. I did the next best thing. I tipped the dregs from one of the barrels over Billy's head. I backed off towards the stairs to watch his reaction. At first it looked as if I was in for a lathering, until the scowl turned into a giggle and then into spluttering laughter.

That's when I saw the half-empty bottle of brandy lying next to him. At the same moment I heard Dan at the top of the cellar steps. I quickly hid the bottle and pulled Billy to his feet.

"Upstairs," Dan said to me. I didn't argue. I could hear the pint pots being banged on the counter. A few minutes later Dan hauled Billy up behind the bar. Billy slumped over the counter as Dan's eyes darted round the room.

"Tom!" he shouted after a second or two. "Some cargo to be delivered, pal."

Tom, the resident taxi driver, nodded and together they got Billy outside. Christ knows what he felt like when he hit the fresh air.

"You'll be covering for him tonight, won't you?" Dan said when he returned. It wasn't a question.

After the pub had shut and I'd done my bit I went round to Billy's house. He was slumped on the sofa where I presumed Tom had dumped him.

First things first. I put the kettle on. The larder was well stocked. I made a plate of cheese and onion sandwiches and a pot of tea. Feed the body and you ease the mind, Grandma Isobel always used to say. She would have taken command of the situation at once with a mixture of tolerance, compassion and hard-headedness. You never knew which side of her would be foremost at any given time, but it invariably turned out to be the most appropriate one. Billy could certainly have benefited from a bit of her slapping and soothing.

We ate in silence. Me out of hunger, him, who knows. By the end of the feed I felt we'd healed the breach. Good habit, breaking bread together.

"I'm sorry about going at you, Bernie," he said quietly.

"I know that," I answered. "Anything I can do before I get back to my hovel?"

"Would you tidy out the bedroom for me? I can't bring myself to go in there with her undies and everything strewn around and I do need a proper sleep."

The bedroom was a mess. Bras, panties, stockings littered the room. Make-up lay like a defeated army all over the utility dressing table. A sweet smell lingered over everything. Bourjois, Evening in Paris. There was a sense of desperation about it all. I didn't think that clearly then, though. I thought, why haven't I got a wardrobe full of clothes and a box of jewellery and where does she get the money from? Billy didn't exactly take home a fat wage. Dan Kavanagh was a fair man, he paid over the odds to his staff, but it was still chicken-feed really.

I set about organising the chaos. By the time I'd picked up all the dirty clothes, the old wicker linen bin was straining. I drew the line at washing it. Billy would have to sort that one out. I was looking under the bed for stray items when I saw the wooden writing box with the multi-coloured butterflies on the lid. I recognised it at once. It had belonged to Isobel and she'd promised it to me when she died. As far as I knew she was still in the land of the living.

I pulled the box out and cautiously lifted the lid as if some concealed demon might attack me. Isobel had always regarded the box as sacred and had once pummelled Deirdre's ears for looking in it. The first thing I saw was an envelope addressed to me in Isobel's handwriting. It had been sent via Deirdre. I looked at the postmark.

Deirdre had had the letter a month! I felt outraged. Even more so when I discovered it had been opened. It read:

> Dearest Bernadette,
> We are all very sad you are staying in that god-forsaken place, it was a very naughty thing you did sneaking away like that without any word to those who love you and pray to God to keep you safe are you alright my dear for we should be mortified to hear bad news I hear tell the likes of you need to stick with your own Catholic Irish I mean if you're not to be getting into troubles. Anyway you'll be needing a sort of talisman to keep you safe so I'm sending you over my writing box I know you always loved it. Colm Connolly is away over there next week and promises to drop it off at Deirdre's for you no point in waiting till I'm dead pet although by the way I feel that day isn't too far off send a line to me dear so that I can have some peace about worrying for you.
> The Blessed Virgin be with you, love.
> Grandma Isobel.

Isobel had never learned much about punctuation or full stops, but her letter still hit me where it hurt. At the same time rage shot through my body like a sudden fever. If Deirdre had been in the house, I think I would have hit her head off a wall until she passed out. Isobel's wasn't the only letter in the box. There was one from Mam asking why I hadn't written back to Isobel and informing me that she was ill. In the face of all this, any sympathy I had with Billy's situation fell away from me.

I'll give him one thing, he didn't try to deny his knowledge of the box and the letters. In fact he admitted that Colm Connolly had wanted to see me and Billy had spun him some tale about me running off to London. I slapped him then. Hard on both cheeks. He didn't try to stop me. As I stormed out of the house with Isobel's box under my arm, I hoped to Christ he was beginning to see the light. Though I wasn't optimistic. His obsession enveloped him like treacle. I decided later that Billy was probably the first masochist I knew. I swore that I would never let myself get into the grip of an obsession; would never want to be with someone who didn't truly want me. I didn't realise what a very lonely furrow I was ploughing for myself, or that God was laughing up His sleeve at me.

SIX

I SPENT THE rest of the afternoon writing letters home, trying to explain the delay in getting in touch without damning Deirdre. I don't know why I still shrank from an outright assault on her. Perhaps I didn't want to cause further grief or perhaps I secretly knew that if push came to shove Deirdre would be the one who would be believed. I had no doubt she would lie quite unashamedly if she had to. I didn't feel strong enough to test my theory out.

The pub was heaving that night. Shoulder to shoulder. I overheard some talk about Waterford at the end of the bar and asked the men if they knew Colm Connolly. They said he'd been in the pub about two weeks previously on his way to see relations in the north-east.

"Any chance he'll be calling back again?" I asked.

"Right enough I think, towards the end of the month probably. Want me to tell him you were asking after him?" Timothy O'Keefe said with an accompanying wink.

I thought about Colm Connolly as I bustled around the bar. I didn't think I'd recognise him if I saw him. We'd lived close by for years, but when he was eight his family moved somewhere up near Athlone to take over a smallholding that had been left to them. I hadn't seen him since their leaving party, but I knew the families had kept in touch.

"Phone call for Billy about Deirdre," Dan said in my ear. I nearly dropped the pint I was pulling. He took it expertly out of my hand and signalled for me to get to the phone. The woman said her name was Louie. She was obviously distressed and all I could get out of her was that someone should come immediately to an address in Selly Oak. I put the phone down slowly and glanced up at the clock. An hour before closing. Dan was watching me when I turned back to the bar. Inside his giant bulk and hard mouth nestled a gentle, inquisitive heart.

"Tom!" he yelled into the corner of the bar where Tom was to be found playing dominoes when he wasn't out taxi driving. The bar was his office. Dan was his only regular customer, having never learned the aggressive art of driving.

"Bernie needs a ride. Take her there and then wait in case she needs to go somewhere else," Dan said out of the corner of his mouth. His Woodbine bobbed up and down as he spoke but he always managed to avoid getting ash in the drinks. I wanted to hug him to show my thanks, but I knew he'd die of embarrassment, so I merely nodded my appreciation of his gesture.

"Hey," he said as I made to leave, "take her to Billy then get the hell out of it."

He was an addict of tough-guy films. I think Robert Mitchum was his role model.

Tom knew the city like he knew his own face. When I gave him the address I noticed his eyebrows lift, just for an instant, then his face assumed its normal bland expression. Dan told me he'd developed the blank look to an art form during a stint in an English prison, but he never elaborated. When we drove up the tree-lined street and came to a halt outside a neat semi-detached house, I think my eyebrows did a dance too.

I noticed Tom kept the engine running as I walked down the path to the side door. I paused before I knocked and began to wonder what the hell I was doing chasing after Deirdre when she'd done nothing but dump on me since I'd arrived. The door was flung open while I stood pondering. The woman – Louie, I presumed – was wearing a flowered dressing gown which swept the floor as she walked. That was all she had on, apart from satin heeled slippers. Everything about her was shades of pink, including her lipstick and her nails, which were about half an inch long.

"She's in there," Louie said, pointing to a door on the right. I could hear music coming from the room directly in front of me, but before I could make out what it was Louie had slammed the door to my right wide open. I was not prepared for what I saw.

Deirdre was lying in a bed with her head hanging over the side towards a bucket. She was vomiting. It sounded as if she'd been doing it for hours. The white sheets were speckled with blood. When Deirdre lifted her face I saw it had come from her mouth, which was cut and swollen, and a gash on her cheekbone just under her left eye. The eye itself was puffed up and almost closed with bruising. I wanted to vomit too. Instead I took Dierdre gently in my arms and made soothing noises as she clung to me, sobbing and gasping for air.

"Who did this?" I asked Louie. She just shook her head
"It happens, that's all," she said eventually. I noticed

her voice shook a little, just like my knees were doing. I started to get up off the bed, fighting a strong urge to hit something. Deirdre clung on to me. A male voice shouted "Louie" from the room with the music. It all seemed terribly unreal and at the same time too real. I began to feel dizzy, lightheaded; beads of sweat bubbled on my upper lip. Then Tom was in the room. He acted like a man who had seen death and spat in its face. Within seconds he had Deirdre wrapped in blankets and was carrying her out of the house. Infected by his calmness I gathered up her clothes, strewn every which way in the room, and located her bag, which had been a birthday present from Billy before their wedding. Louie was still leaning in the doorway and the music was still playing.

"I'll be back," I promised her as I swept past her.

"Give my love to Dan," she replied.

"Dan?" I said, but she just shrugged her shoulders. I could see behind the casual façade. She was shaken and scared. I closed the outside door behind me and paused to get a deep breath of air. Tom had laid Deirdre out on the back seat of his Ford. He was holding her hand and crooning softly to her.

"Can you drive?" he asked me as I stepped up. I shook my head. "Well I'd better teach you then, because one day it might save your life. But not tonight. Hop in the back and keep her steady."

Tom turned and drove the car as gently as the machine itself would allow. I could see him checking on us in his rear mirror all the time. We were pulling up outside Billy's place in a matter of minutes.

"But we should get her to a hospital," I protested.

Deirdre moaned and Tom shook his head slowly.

"I know what I'm doing, don't you worry. I've a cousin over in Wolverhampton who's a nurse; she'll come back with me and check things out." He started to lift Deirdre out of the car. I began arguing again, but it was useless, he just ignored me. I was definitely in over my head. What had Dan said: get the hell out of it. When Billy opened the door I knew that's exactly what I should do. He looked like someone had just told him he'd won a fortune. I followed him into the house feeling wretched and angry and all sorts of other confused emotions. Billy was clearly so overjoyed to have Deirdre back that her injuries, her damage, meant nothing to him. He didn't even ask how it had happened.

"Come on," Tom said quietly. "I'll drop you back at the pub on my way to Wolverhampton. There's nothing you can do here."

I took Deirdre's hand and kissed it before I left. I promised I'd call and see her the following day. She tried to smile, but it hurt her too much. I'm willing to bet that it would have been the most sincere smile she'd ever given me if she could have managed it. All my anger about her and Jake tumbled away. She was my sister and she needed me.

The regulars were just leaving as we arrived back at the pub. We'd been gone less than an hour, but I felt as if I'd gone through a whole night of torment.

"You've been to that house before, haven't you, Tom?" I asked.

"Leave it alone now, Bernadette," Tom replied.

I felt like a child who was being humoured by an

indulgent parent, and I didn't like it. I almost stamped my foot in frustration. "So has Dan, hasn't he?" I insisted.

"There'll be time enough to talk tomorrow when you visit Deirdre. Leave it alone till then." Tom smiled as he waved goodbye. It was a kind smile, I thought, but I was beginning to doubt my ability to judge those sorts of things.

Dan was sluicing the toilets out while singing "The Wild Colonial Boy". That was usually my first job each morning. He'd washed the tables down as well. I was moved by his kindness and so distressed by the evening's events that I stood and bawled. Dan immediately put his arms around me. We stood for at least ten minutes like that until the crying died away to be replaced by hiccoughs. I smiled up at him with relief and gratitude and realised with a start that Dad had never ever showed me such tenderness. I also understood how much I'd concealed my longing for it.

"I'll put the kettle on," I said. We looked at each other for a second or two and realised that we'd crossed some invisible hurdle together.

"Tell me about Tom," I asked as we drank our tea in the empty bar.

"What's there to tell?" he replied. "You either like him or you don't."

"I want to know where he comes from; what he believes in; why he runs his business from your bar; why he's so often silent."

"Christ but you're a nosey little devil, aren't you?" he said. "I've heard you in the bar with the customers giving it hell with interrogations. I'll bet you were born with a question on your tongue."

I drank some tea and watched Dan's eyes. They were sharp, concentrating, in spite of his casual air.

"And you're very good at avoiding giving answers, if I might say so," I retaliated.

"Tom will tell you what he wants you to know, okay?" he said.

I knew I would get no further with my enquiries about Tom. I had found out that there was loyalty between the two men.

"Are you planning to stay on over here?" Dan asked awkwardly, as if he wasn't used to prying.

"There's nothing for me to go back to."

"Your Mam and Da will be missing you, won't they? Maybe they need a helping hand."

I drank a little more tea before replying, getting even for his tight-lippedness about Tom.

"I don't think so. Glad to see the back of me."

"Was there a disagreement or something?" he continued. I sighed, not really having any answers neatly to hand.

"I just don't think they like me particularly," I said quietly, realising there was a choke in my voice.

"It happens," he said softly. "I've seen it before. Well, that's good news for me anyway. My best barmaid isn't planning on leaving me in the lurch." He took my hand and squeezed it. I felt comforted and wary at the same time.

SEVEN

I SLEPT LIKE an arthritic dog, tossing and turning, running up dead-end streets, seeing distorted images of myself in a hall of mirrors. I was late getting up for work, which earned me a familiar scowl from Dan. That pleased me. Our few moments of closeness the night before weren't going to change anything.

I worked like crazy to make up for the lost time, eager to prove my dependability. I watched Dan on the quiet, somehow seeing him differently. The thatch of blue-black hair, heavy eyebrows, lined, angular face with tell-tale signs of a boxing past. I had no idea how old he was, somewhere around fifty I supposed, and no idea if there had ever been a Mrs Kavanagh. I didn't even know how long he'd been in England, and yet at that moment I felt closer to him than anyone else in the world. I'm sure Freud would have had some conclusions to draw from it. I certainly did. I wanted to know why my Mam and Dad had never made me feel safe and cared for in that way. Wasn't that what they were supposed to do?

Supposition, is it? God said. Thesis. Field of inquiry. My but you're getting awful verbal, aren't you? He sounded so much like Father Molloy at times.

Opening time brought trouble. Two policemen strolled in just as the first pints were being pulled. They have a way with them. They are immediately intimidating, even for the most innocent. I sensed a communal sigh as they approached the bar.

Dan bristled but put on his polite façade. It didn't help much, because it was almost identical to his aggressive one. Only those who knew him well could tell the difference.

"Morning, Mr Kavanagh," the tallest one said. His face looked as if it was being sucked slowly inwards from a point directly behind his nose. His pal with the red hair just nodded slowly like a branch in the wind. "We're looking for a Mr Tom O'Neill. I understand he frequents this place."

I had been briefed from my first day about police and any other unknown people asking questions. Say nothing. I watched Dan doing his say-nothing routine. It consisted of shifting about from one foot to the other, scratching his head and coughing every so often. The customers stayed away from the bar while this went on, and if either policeman looked towards them they pointedly turned their backs. There was a long history to this attitude, in part to do with memories of the Black and Tans and in part to do with personal experiences of being treated like thick scum. A favourite subject for English jokes. Grandma Isobel always used to say that prejudice of any sort is based on fear. I wonder what the English were frightened of? Their own history in Ireland? These two didn't look all that fearful; they looked like they were having a great time. Dan's tolerance was being stretched like tired elastic. Just at that point Jake came bouncing in, swiftly followed by Timothy O'Keefe. They stopped short when they saw the police, turned tail and did a runner. The police were after them like dogs at a race-track. The pub clientele heaved up to the bar grinning from ear to ear. It was the first time I'd seen Jake since handing him my virginity. Our eyes had only locked for a second, but it had been enough time to feel my thighs sizzle.

After we'd filled up the empty glasses I made tea for me and Dan. "What was that all about?" I asked as we sipped the dark orange liquid.

"Nothing to do with you. You just keep your eyes and ears shut round here and you'll be fine."

"Is Tom in trouble?" I persisted.

Dan ignored this and my next two attempts. I went in the back to start making the sandwiches, which would soon be in demand. I was getting sick and tired of being told to mind my place. That wasn't what I'd come to England for. But then I was beginning to wonder what exactly I had come for. Fairy tales about independence and a high living to be made seemed grossly exaggerated. Dan poked his head round the door.

"Two cheese and onion," he said. I didn't look up but I knew his head was still round the doorway. "It's for your own good, Bernie. The less you know, the less to hurt you."

"Ignorance is bliss, you mean!" I snapped. "Well, sod that." He looked at me deadly serious for a second then burst into laughter. I could still hear him chuckling when I'd finished the order. I stormed in with it and banged it down on the bar counter.

"Service required in the snug," Dan said quietly. It was Jake and another lad I'd never seen before. He nearly jumped out of his skin when I got Jake by the throat and pushed his head against the back of the bench.

It surprised me as well. My reactions to Jake continually surprised me.

"Did you have anything to do with what happened to Deirdre last night?" I spat at him. He easily freed himself from my grip and shrugged his jacket down.

"You know I didn't," he said. "How could you think that?" His eyes told me I'd hurt him. Maybe that's what I'd intended.

"That's right enough," his pal said. "He was with me all evening." I told him to clear off. It was wasted breath. As I faced Jake I felt the other lad's hand spread across my backside, roving, then pinching. "You available at the same rate as your sister or do I get a discount from knowing Jake?" he said with a snigger.

I don't know what I would have done when I recovered from my shock, but it was all done for me. Jake grabbed him and bashed his head down on the table. Dan rushed in and booted the pair of them into the street. I heard him telling Jake not to bring his pal back or he'd be banned. Dan's threats were always enforced, so I was sure that was the last I'd see of him. It never pays to be so sure. Jake's departure had left me with a pain in my ribcage. It wasn't indigestion.

Billy arrived soon after, glowing and ready to take on the world. I felt sick thinking about what must go on in his head.

"Deirdre says thanks for last night but she doesn't want you to come round today," he said chirpily.

"That's a shame because I am going round and there's damn all you can do to stop me," I replied.

Billy started to argue but Dan shouted from the bar,

"Get in here, Billy, you're half an hour late as it is."

I only had a few bob left until pay-day, so I decided to walk to see Deirdre and feed myself out of her pantry. Mine held two ends of a loaf and a dribble of milk. I became more determined with every step I took. I was going to get to the bottom of it all. Deirdre wouldn't fob me off like everyone else. Even though I felt sorry about her hurt, I still felt upset about the writing box and the rest.

It was a miserable day, grey and damp, but there was optimism in the air. Eden was out. Macmillan was in. Polygamy was abolished in Tunisia. I hadn't yet caught the Asian flu that was sweeping the country. However, Britain had exploded its first hydrogen bomb in the Pacific and Russia had launched Sputnik 1 and 2. Maybe that accounted for the bad weather. I would have to ask Dan, who collected these facts like a magpie does shiny objects.

In spite of all his experience as an Irishman in England, all his battles with Catholicism and all the pessimism and desperation he witnessed daily in the pub, Dan remained essentially an optimist. He had great faith in the positive potential of human beings.

Louie answered Deirdre's door. I could smell the booze as soon as she opened her mouth to grin at me. Her teeth were smeared with bright red lipstick.

"Oh," she giggled, "it's the Good Samaritan sister . . . come in, have a drink . . . and while we're at it, why not crack your face and give us a smile?"

I brushed past her and rushed into Deirdre's bedroom. She was in bed, propped up with cushions and pillows. Jake was stretched out on top of it. The gin bottle on the dressing table was nearly empty and the whole place reeked of Evening in Paris. They were laughing when I walked in, and something which hurt like an open wound made me feel certain that I was the subject of their mirth. Of course it could have been guilt and paranoia. That and the fact that Jake wouldn't meet my eye and seemed to be trying to make himself as small as possible. Deirdre noticed his discomfort too. She gave me such a corrosive look I felt my skin pucker in defence.

— EIGHT —

JAKE JUMPED OFF the bed and brushed himself down. "Oh, I see, little Miss Prim arrives and everyone suddenly clams up eh? Well fuck it, she doesn't worry me," Louie said, reaching for the gin bottle. I don't remember clearly what I was thinking; it was all so mixed up with my feelings for Jake and Deirdre. I know I was surprised at Louie's suggestion that either of them might be bothered about my opinions.

"Didn't you get my message?" Deirdre asked.

"I got it all right," I said.

"So?"

"So I've got a few questions I'd like answered."

"Indeed."

Jake was fidgeting about to the left of the bed. Deirdre and I looked at him at the same moment, her willing him to stay, me wishing he would leave. Louie continued to drink.

"I'll make some tea then," Jake said at last. He scuttled off to the kitchen, swiftly followed by Louie stumbling on her high heels. Deirdre's face had taken on that familiar sneer which she seemed to reserve especially for me. The bruising and swelling made her look even more hostile.

I sat on the side of the bed in an attempt to bridge the distance between us.

"I'm grateful for last night," she finally said, "but I

don't know what else you want off me." My face must have
given away my surprise. "And . . . and," she continued,
"the thing about the writing box and letters was all just
a mistake . . . I'd been away and then I forgot and . . ."

I interrupted her at this stage. There was something
dreadfully embarrassing about Deirdre trying to apologise.

"Don't bother, Deirdre. I know fine well you're lying.
What I don't know is why, and what I want to know is
what happened to you?"

Deirdre started examining her hands as if she'd never
seen them before, then she played with the bedcovers. I
looked around the room, waiting. It was garishly deco-
rated in reds and golds, imitation posh stuff, with trinkets
everywhere. The eiderdown was a deep crimson colour
embroidered with large blue-and-lemon swirls. It would
be Deirdre's taste, because Billy didn't have any strong
likes and dislikes in the face of her desires. I knew (from
articles Dan had read to me) that the décor of a room told
you a lot about the person who'd done it, but all I could
read into this was that she was a bit of a mess. I knew
that already.

"Look," she said, "things like that happen all the time.
People lose their temper and regret it afterwards, and
that's all there is to know. And there was no need to go
accusing Jake."

"What were you doing at that house?"

"Visiting Louie. Is that not allowed?"

"What was Louie doing walking round half-naked
while you were supposed to be visiting her?" Deirdre
looked past me at the doorway. Louie was leaning there.
I don't know how long she'd been there and at that

moment I didn't care.

"Not that it's any of your damn business, but just so as you'll give Deirdre a break, I'll tell you," she said shakily.

There was a part of me that knew what it was she was going to tell me. There was a part of me that wanted to know and another frightened me that didn't want to know. I was torn between running away and hiding from the reality of it and a need to face facts and maybe understand something.

Louie sat on the edge of the armchair. Her neat suit was smeared with ash where she'd been careless with her cigarettes. She suddenly looked very small.

"The house belongs to a man, a cousin of mine. I can stay there as long as I earn enough to give him a cut. He decides what is enough and he sends the customers. I . . . I just give them what they want . . . which is sex in all sorts of shapes and forms."

I half-listened while Louie continued her story about pregnancy at sixteen; being thrown out by her parents; her desire to provide for her daughter; the offer her cousin made when she was in dire need. Deirdre sat perfectly still through it all, aware that I would be making the connections about her and the house. I felt cold and scared as Louie finished her tale.

I heard the chink of cups and turned to see Jake standing in the doorway. He took in the scene in the bedroom, put the tray on the dressing table and left. A few seconds later I heard the outside door close softly.

I felt more alone than any time since I'd arrived with my high ideals and big expectations. I felt excluded from the company of Deirdre and Louie, and somehow the problem all seemed to be of my own making.

"Satisfied now?" Deirdre asked.

I couldn't respond.

"Course she is," Louie chipped in. "That's what she wanted to hear. Now she can go off all high and mighty."

I poured tea for us all so as to stop feeling like a spare part. Louie offered me a cigarette. I took it. Why not? It made me feel sick but that was better than feeling numb.

"Wasn't there any other way?" I asked.

"Not at that particular time. Not a way that would let me be with Nancy, my little girl, when I needed to. There was only me to look after her . . . Now . . . well Nancy's eight and maybe I could do something else, but it's not that easy . . . The money is good." She paused and looked around the room. "I'm saving to get a nice place for me and Nancy and make sure she goes to a good school and has a proper chance in life."

"Doesn't Nancy know what's going on?"

"NO!" she yelled. "I'm very careful. What do you take me for?"

All three of us grasped the humour in Louie's remark. Our laughter released some of the tension that had built up.

Deirdre suddenly started shivering and snuggled into bed. I sat on the side of it.

"I thought you'd have run off screaming by now, or at least started insulting me," Deirdre said.

"Do you really think I'm that unfeeling, that cold?"

"You always have been. I got more love than you from Mam and Dad, but you were the one who always coped; who never demanded more; who let me be the brat of the house always sounding like a spoilt little shite next to you who took everything in your stride. Mam and Dad would have preferred you to be the wretch of the pack, then they could have justified their dislike. But no, you were the model child, weren't you?"

"Why didn't they like me, Deirdre?"

"You're not easy to like . . ." The flat door slammed shut and Billy shouted that he was home. Deirdre gave me a look that could have been a plea, and Louie swept the gin bottle into her bag as she picked up her coat. Billy stared at us with a sort of incomprehension written on his features. He wanted to be alone with his wife, the expression said.

"I'll walk along with you," Louie said as she grasped my arm. Deirdre had put on her little girl mask.

Outside, the September air was sharp and biting, but the sky was bright. Louie shivered. Her clothes weren't warm enough for the weather. Her ankles looked blue.

"Don't judge Deirdre too quickly," she said as we reached the main road. "She's been good to me and she did try other work first. Billy's never going to make anything of himself, is he? Deirdre wants nice things, so she's got to get them for herself."

She waved as she headed in the opposite direction for her bus.

I had an hour before I started work again. Time enough to walk back, swallow a pint of tea and get to it. There was a lot more still to be said, a lot more questions to be asked, but I felt I'd made a start. Perhaps me and Deirdre would learn to like one another after all. He that increaseth knowledge increaseth sorrow, God said.

A car pulled up beside me. I got ready to yell abuse at

whoever was attempting to pick me up. It was Tom. He opened the passenger door and leaned across.

"Time for your first driving lesson," he said.

It was the last thing I felt like doing. I wanted to luxuriate in self-pity and stick knitting needles into a clay model of Jake.

"There's not enough time."

"Oh aye, there is. Dan's had to go out and said to tell you he won't be back till five. So you've got an hour you didn't know you had." He was very determined.

"How'd you know where to find me?" I asked as we sped out towards the Lickey Hills.

"Finger on the pulse all the time," he laughed. I looked very sceptical.

The car was an Austin 7, chunky and green. It felt responsive, almost human, and smelled like Father Molloy's old jalopy, whatever that was. I got a real stir of excitement being behind the wheel, an adrenalin surge. Being in control, that's what I needed.

It wasn't a real taxi, of course, just the odd-job car attached to the pub, but Tom had found a "FOR HIRE/ON HIRE" sign from somewhere and proudly displayed it on the dashboard, permanently "ON HIRE".

— NINE —

TOM DECIDED I was a natural for driving. He said it was a pleasure teaching me. I asked how to go about getting legal, but he just shrugged his shoulders. If I wanted to be above-board I'd have to find out for myself. I found out much later that he'd never passed his test but had taken over the licence and name of a pal who'd gone back to Ireland.

Things slugged along for the next few weeks. I didn't see Deirdre but got daily progress reports from Billy, who wanted to keep her housebound as long as he could. Jake stayed away from the pub. I did go and visit Louie though. Tom dropped me off after one of our lessons.

She had a couple of hours to spare between clients and was fresh out of the bath when I got there. With her face scrubbed and her fair hair combed back off her face, I realised that she was much younger than I'd thought.

"Twenty-four," she told me when I asked her. "But I feel much older sometimes. It's this trade; makes you see life differently." I nodded, content for her to talk on. "I used to look up to men, respect them, think they were much stronger than me, but now . . ." She left the phrase unfinished. I discovered that she'd actually been born and brought up in the south, where her parents ran a corner shop. For them, what the neighbours thought was far more important than anything else. When Louie got pregnant she had to be banished so that her parents could save face. Her mother had softened a bit over the years, but her father had never forgiven her. If they found out about the prostitution Louie felt certain they'd hand her over to the police themselves.

"When I go and visit them," she said, "my father makes a pot of tea, but he only ever puts two cups and saucers on the tray. One for himself and one for my mother. It's as if he can't bear to acknowledge my existence. He ignores Nancy completely. Thank God for Dan Kavanagh; otherwise she wouldn't have any idea what a grandfather was supposed to be like."

"Dan?"

"Yeah, it was Dan's son Kieron who did the dirty on me and ran off."

"I thought . . ."

"I know. Dan told me that since you found out about me being on the job you've been very cool towards him. You thought he was coming round here for that, didn't you?"

I felt ashamed that I'd jumped so quickly to that conclusion. Louie was grinning when I looked back at her.

"It's all right," she said.

The doorbell rang and Louie jumped. "That'll be Nancy. I have her brought home in a taxi."

Nancy had her mother's fair hair, but it reached down to her backside. Her eyes were more green than blue, shining out of a pale Celtic complexion. I could imagine a little of what Kieron must have looked like. I didn't know much about children, but she seemed very serious for an eight-year-old. She kissed Louie, smiled briefly at me, then disappeared upstairs to change out of her school uniform.

Louie started busying herself in the kitchen, making Nancy's tea. She invited me to stay, but I said I'd better get back. I wanted to let them have their time together.

The bus was crowded on the way back to the city. Shift workers chain smoking, looking grey from sleep, making their way to factories on the north side. Women with too many children trying to keep control and looking as if all they wanted to do was sleep. Girls giggling together about boyfriends and parties. I knew what Louie meant about feeling old. I sometimes felt I'd been born old.

I looked around at the young girls and wondered what had happened to my coming of age. It was as if I'd gone from child to adult in a space of weeks, with no real preparation; with no one giving me the benefit of any experience.

A woman opposite me was reading a magazine. One of the adverts facing me said that "Every woman, everywhere, needs a deodorant. Mum cream prevents odour, does not stop perspiration." It all seemed so alien. The truth of it was that I didn't fit back home and I didn't fit here. But whether that was the nature of being an immigrant or an oddness within me, I was yet to discover. The city with all its noise and hustle sped past me, an unwilling adult who often couldn't remember ever being a child.

Say six Hail Marys, God said in an authoritative voice. It'll make you feel better. I did and it didn't. So much for Him.

I began to feel depressed thinking about it all, wondering at the whys and wherefores of everything, as Father

Molloy used to say. I knew I was having to learn things
at too fast a pace and that maybe I was only half-absorbing
everything. Like the idea of Deirdre and Louie being
prostitutes. What did it really mean to me? Apart from a
few gropings back home and the shedding of my virginity
with Jake, I was in complete ignorance of the complexities
of sex. Part of me had a desire to explore and discover,
and the rest of me reared up in horror at the very idea of it.

God had a lot to do with it. Or was it Jesus? How come
He never had adolescent urges? But of course He did; it's
just that we weren't told about them. And what about the
fetish of letting Mary Magdalen wash His feet and dry
them with her hair! What was that all about? She was
showing contrition for her sins, God replied, just as you
should be. I stopped listening.

There were feelings that Dan Kavanagh stirred in me,
but I wouldn't let them come to the surface. I was afraid
of his age, his experience and the fact that he felt like a
dad should feel. I found it impossible to distinguish
between my affection for him and urges which might be
sexual. I wondered about asking Louie for advice, but
sex seemed such a matter-of-fact thing to her that I felt
she wouldn't really be able to help me. Why was it all so
confusing? Because it's more fun for Me that way, God
replied, which was probably the truth.

Thinking about Deirdre got me thinking about Billy.
I'd felt such sympathy with him before, but now I didn't
know what I felt, except a sort of exasperation. He
irritated me with his whining attitude towards things, his
insular approach to life. I couldn't deny Deirdre had used
him blatantly to get to England, but she could have left

him high and dry once she got here. Did she need his possessiveness, his adulation, to bolster her own shaky self-image? Strange to feel old and yet innocent at the same time.

Dan and I had taken to eating together every so often, and when I got back he had a huge stew with dumplings bubbling on the stove. It smelled lovely. He'd also given me the run of the living room, so that now we operated more like family than landlord and tenant.

"I'm sorry about thinking you were . . . about you and Louie," I said softly as we sat down to eat. He grinned and held out his hand. We shook. The food was great and Dan entertained me as usual with items from the paper. Paintings by apes exhibited at the Institute of Contemporary Arts. A new, exciting novel by a young man called John Braine called *Room at the Top*. A musical being made of Shaw's *Pygmalion* called *My Fair Lady*.

"Terrible name for it, don't you think?" Dan asked. I admitted I hadn't read nor even heard of the book so had no opinion on the title. "My girl," he said severely, "someone should take your education in hand before it's too late. I've a pal up in Yorkshire who sends me down books to read. You'd like him; he's a self-educated man, a budding communist and a laugh a minute." Dan fetched a cardboard box from his bedroom. It held about a dozen books.

"Here now, pick one of these to start off with. Make it a big one," he said, directing my attention to the largest book in the box. It was *The Ragged Trousered Philanthropist* by Robert Tressel. "Now we'll see what stuff you're made of," he beamed.

Opening time found the police with us again. The same two. I found out this time that they were called Smith (the tall one) and Hawkins (red hair).

"Have you nothing better to do with your time than harass innocent landlords?" Dan said. "There's surely death and destruction going on somewhere out there while you loiter in here."

"Very humorous, Mr Kavanagh," Smith replied. "But if we got some co-operation from the likes of you it would make life easier. Now, about that crook Maloney who ran off the other day." Dan had gone on to blank-expression time.

"He's talking about your pal Jake, the ladies' man," Hawkins said to me. I was so shocked to be addressed that I blushed. Smith and Hawkins thought that was funny.

"Never seen an Irish tart blush before, have you, Hawkins?" Smith said. I looked at Dan, knowing they were trying to rile him. I saw his left eyebrow twitch just a little. All at once the seven customers who had been biding their time over a second pint emptied their glasses and piled up to the bar. Smith and Hawkins were surrounded and they looked uncomfortable. I was pleased. Pleased also to see the anxiety leave Dan's face.

Smith and Hawkins left with parting shots about thieves and thugs and all Micks being tarred with the same brush. As they reached the side door they bumped into a well-dressed, older man who blocked their passage. He ushered them back into the room with a nod of his head.

"I think you boys should apologise to Mr Kavanagh for such slack-mouthed insults. What do you say?" the

man said. Smith and Hawkins mumbled something which
could have been "Sorry" and rushed off without glancing
back. The man and Dan slapped hands together across
the bar counter and cracked up laughing.

"Chief Inspector Molloy, CID," Dan introduced him
to me. "Born in County Waterford. Not too far from
your patch."

"Not related to Father Molloy?" I asked as I shook
hands.

"The very same. My Uncle Patrick, the old sourpuss."

"I never knew he had family over here," I said, eager
to dig the dirt on God's representative on earth.

"The renegade section," Molloy replied with a chuckle.
"Every one of us heathens and a lost cause. I believe he
personally requested our excommunication from the
Church. Had his reputation to consider. Though, from
what I hear through the grapevine, there are one or two
skeletons in his own cupboard."

My mind immediately jumped to an image of Father
Molloy and Molly Cahill in bed together, but for the life
of me I couldn't imagine him with no clothes on. There's
hope for you yet then, God said. I ignored His interruption.

I asked Molloy a lot of questions and found him very
open and friendly. He was curious about me too, a rare
occurrence for an attractive man, they're so often
wrapped up in themselves. I began to suspect he was
flirting in a very mild way when Dan suggested I might
make myself busy behind the bar.

"Sorry about Smith and Hawkins," Molloy said to
Dan. "They're eager to make a name for themselves and
they'd like to do it on my patch. Get one over on the

Paddies, you know the sort of thing."

Dan nodded as he poured a Scotch and soda for Molloy, who signalled for Dan to join him in the snug. Billy arrived shortly afterwards, and as the bar was quiet I had a few games of dominoes with Tom.

Billy was no longer triumphant, I could see that immediately, but I refused to pander to him. He only ever wanted my ear when Deirdre was playing up. The rest of the time he treated me like part of the furniture. He managed to collar me at the end of the night as we cleaned the tables.

"Bernie," he whined, "she's gone again. The bloke in the flat upstairs said she went off in a taxi about six. I'd just gone up to the off-licence to get her some fags."

"What do want me to do, Billy?"

"Go round to Louie's and talk her into coming back. Will you?"

"No, Billy, I won't. It's not up to me what you and Deirdre do. I'm not her bloody guardian angel or yours." Before he could get any more whingeing in Dan appeared, ready to lock up.

"The kettle's on upstairs," he said to me. I left him to show Billy the door.

Dan was smiling when he came up but he soon turned serious. "That lad who was with Jake the other evening when the coppers were in." I nodded. "Know anything about him?"

"Only that he was a prize knacker. Never seen him before that night."

"Molloy reckons he's bad trouble. Hangs around with Irish lads and pulls them in on thieving jobs, then leaves them in the shit. Reckons he's got some sort of deal on with Smith and Hawkins whereby the Irish lads get nicked and he gets a cut of the takings. Nasty business. You might want to warn Jake to steer clear."

"I might."

"Still suffering from hurt pride, are we?"

"I wouldn't call it that."

"No, but I would," he said. "Get on to bed and start your education. It'll help get things in some sort of perspective."

"So said the wise old man," I sneered. Dan laughed. I went to bed.

I read some of the Tressel and found that Dan was right, it did help to get things into some sort of perspective. Mind you, it didn't make the depression go away. Writing to Joan helped and I began hatching a plan to get Dan and Joan together and create a whole new family for myself. The fact that he didn't talk about his past relationships at all allowed me the freedom to develop some romantic illusions about lost loves and passions. Then I'd remember shithead Kieron and the leaving of Louie and Nancy. Chip off the old block? No, I had to trust my instincts, Dan was essentially a good man. And what the devil would you know about good and bad? God sneered. You're just off the cattle boat and as green as can be. Does Dan Kavanagh go to church? Does he take communion? When was his last confession? His soul is definitely not in a state of grace. Neither is mine, I replied. True enough, He said, but at least you're still listening to me. At which point I turned over and went to sleep.

— TEN —

ABOUT THREE IN the morning I was woken by a soft thudding. It sounded like someone walking across the floor towards my bed. I turned slowly and gasped before a hand went over my mouth. I could see by the light of the lamppost outside my window that it was the shitty lad who'd been with Jake, the one Molloy had warned us about. He was grinning down at me as he started pulling the bedclothes off. I shivered with cold and panic. Someone else was in the room. I could sense a person over by the door as if standing guard. My mind was darting about trying to think what I could do. I was wearing pyjamas, a cardigan and socks in bed because the room was so cold. Shitface was having trouble undressing me as I resisted all his manoeuvres.

"Come over and hold her down," he hissed at his pal. I saw the shadow shake its head in refusal. "Come on, it'll only take a few minutes."

He loosened his grip for a second as he turned to plead with his man. I pulled my knees up as hard as I could and shoved for all I was worth. It was enough to topple him on to the floor off the narrow bed. I caught my breath and screamed as I ran for the window. I heard the thump of Dan's feet as he responded to the noise. Shitface and his pal ran like ferrets after rabbits. As Dan burst into my room I heard the street door slam shut.

Dan barely had time to help me back to bed and ask me what had happened before there was a hammering on the downstairs door. He padded over to the window, pulled it open and bellowed down into the darkness.

"Who the hell is it?"

The reply came back loud and clear. "Police, Mr Kavanagh. Open up please; we have a warrant to search the premises."

For a second or two there I fondly imagined that they'd come in response to my scream. No such luck. Everything happened swiftly then and in something of a haze. There was shouting, arguing, threats of blows. Dan was hustled off to the cop shop together with a suitcase of stolen jewellery they'd "found" hidden under one of the bench seats in the snug. It was a set-up. Everyone but the two young constables with Smith and Hawkins knew that, and they'd soon learn to keep their mouths shut if they wanted to progress in the force.

I stood shivering in the kitchen after they'd all gone. Shock? Reaction? Cold? A combination of all these. Dan had mouthed for me to phone Molloy, but I had no idea where to contact him. I waited for the kettle to boil and tried to use my dumb brain. Louie answered the phone on the third ring.

"Bernie, I'm working, time is money. Is it urgent?" she said. I wanted to tell her I needed cuddling and comforting but I couldn't. Instead I asked if Deirdre was there. "She's working too." I put the phone down and sat feeling sorry for myself until the kettle started whistling.

After much trial and error and thumbing through the phone book, I located Molloy in Moseley. He promised to get on to it straight away. With that done I sat at the kitchen table smoking one of Dan's Woodbines until I started to vomit. It was while I was in the lavatory that I got a sudden rush of fear wondering if Shitface might come back. As if to confirm my anxiety I heard a creaking noise and knew that someone was making their way upstairs.

I picked up the wooden lavatory brush, the only possible weapon in sight, and crept on to the landing just as the light was switched on. It was Jake. He grinned when he saw the brush in my hand.

"Bit late for cleaning I'd have thought," he said.

"What are you doing here and how the hell did you get in?" I shouted at him, while at the same time fighting down the next wave of vomit. The vomit won. Jake hustled me back to bed while he cleaned it up and made fresh, strong tea.

"Louie sent me," he explained as I sipped. "She thought you sounded in a bit of a state."

I didn't bother to try and understand how Louie would know where to contact Jake at four in the morning. Instead I poured out the night's events, in an incoherent babble by the looks of the expression on Jake's face. He kept stopping me to try and make some sense of it all. When I burst into tears he put his arm around me, but I pulled away suddenly aware that I couldn't trust my reactions when he was close. It was a sobering thought.

"You can go now," I said crisply. "I'm all right."

"Sure you are," he said. "And I'm Parnell reincarnated. Let's see who can tell the biggest lies, shall we? I'll start. First, I don't want to sleep with you." I smiled in spite of myself. "Second, you don't want to sleep with me."

But I did, and I did. This time it was slower, less intense, more fun. This time we fell straight to sleep afterwards wrapped together until we were so hot we had to pull away.

I left Jake sleeping when I heard Dan return about eight. He looked washed out but not defeated.

"You look awful," I said.

"You speak for yourself," he replied. I looked in the kitchen mirror to see my hair sticking up every which way. "I see I needn't have wasted my time worrying about you," he continued. "You clearly weren't worrying about me."

"That's not fair."

"Nothing ever is. Will you make us a pan of porridge while I have a bath and I'll forgive you. Then I'll tell you the tale of Smith and Hawkins."

Jake left while Dan had his bath. He looked uncomfortable, embarrassed. The aftermath.

The tale of Smith and Hawkins was easy to tell, but it had no ending. Molloy was doing all he could, but Dan didn't know if it would be good enough. His best hope was to locate Shitface, get him on an attempted rape charge and offer to bargain for information on the set-up. My mouth dropped open.

"You did realise that they planted the stuff before he tried it on with you?" Dan said in response to my face.

"Yes," I replied. "And I want him punished for what he tried to do to me." Dan looked embarrassed. He started clearing the table in order to hide it.

"Course you want him done," he said, almost to himself.

Work intervened, including whingeing Billy, who nearly got a pint over his head at one point. In the end Dan sent him down to the cellar for an hour to give us both a bit of peace. I wondered if I'd find him with a half-empty bottle of brandy at opening time. His problem, not mine.

Billy didn't want to go home at closing time. He said he couldn't face the empty house. Dan shrugged and told him he'd have to stay in the bar in that case, as he was expecting company. Nancy arrived by taxi a few minutes later. She'd been to the dentist and looked fragile. Dan made custard and gave it to her with tinned peaches. She brightened up in no time.

"I'm off to see Deirdre," I said. "See you later."

Dan followed me into the hall. "You can be remarkably thick at times, Bernie," he said. "Why do you think I'm childminding if it's not so that Louie and Deirdre can work? Go up and read your book like a good girl."

"Oh, sod the book!" I said.

I don't know why I felt so angry. Maybe thinking about what was happening in that neat semi in Selly Oak. Maybe wondering what I was doing continuing with the can of worms that was Jake Maloney. Maybe angry at myself for not stopping to think things through.

I wandered over to the bus station café thinking I might as well join all the other misfits who seemed to congregate there. The coffee was too weak and milky for my liking, but I drank it anyway. There's something about travel centres. They make me feel restless, as if I should be moving on. I watched the travellers struggling with bags and children and listened to the names of the other towns and cities, trying to imagine what they'd be like.

Advertisements on the walls told me that "Drene is the shampoo the film stars use" and also that "He'll never say

'farewell' while you wear Furwul Thistledown Angora".
I wondered whether anyone actually believed the slogans.
They represented such a neat, attractive world, and yet
not so many miles away sex in various forms was being
sought and paid for by "respectable" men. What was it
with these men and sex? Was it a reaction, the aftermath
of war, or something deeper, hidden, unspoken?

The area was booming. Car factories, car components,
work galore. And yes, a wide and varied lot of customers
for Deirdre, Louie and all the other "service industries".
West Indian, African and Asian men who had volun-
teered to fight for the "mother country" in the army and
RAF were now doing shit jobs along with the rest of the
immigrants who'd been recruited from the empire. They,
like the regulars in the pub, talked of working for a short
while before going home. Forty, fifty years later most of
them would still be here.

I got a shock when I went to use the toilet. Shitface was
at the ticket counter! I nearly turned heel and ran to find
Dan but changed my mind. I couldn't keep expecting
other people to sort things out. The logical thing to do
was try and find out where he was going to and what
time his bus left. I slipped into the queue three places
behind him just in time to hear the ticket man say, "Stand
G at four-thirty." Shitface moved furtively towards the
café. Thank Christ I'd wanted a pee at that particular
moment! Don't mention it, God said, all part of the service.

I turned to go back to the pub and there was Jake
blocking the way.

"Leave this to me, Bernie," he said sharply. "You get
yourself out of the way."

More orders. I bristled.

"But you don't understand," I said. "Molloy needs him so that he can make a deal with Smith and Hawkins."

"Becoming quite the expert." He grinned, but it was mirthless. "Molloy shall have him all right, but not until I've finished with him. Anyway, he'll be more open to persuasion in a little while."

I left. There didn't seem any point in doing anything else. Part of me was glad that Shitface was going to get treated in kind for what he had done to me. Another part wondered if that was really the solution to the problem. Typical response. Nothing's certain but uncertainty. I decided to go to bed for an hour, but Dan brought up a pot of tea just as my head hit the pillow. I told him about the scene in the bus station and saw satisfaction spread across his face. It was like the sun coming out. He left quickly to see to Nancy but told me to sleep on as long as I liked because he'd make sure Billy earned his pay that evening. I slept and woke in fits and starts and ended up reading the Tressel book in spite of myself.

What was it that made some people likeable and others hateful? Had Smith and Hawkins had some terrible childhood experience of Irish people or were they merely opportunists, jumping on whatever prejudice was in fashion? There's no doubt that some of Dan's customers were stupid and argumentative and arrogant, and there were among them some from Waterford. No race or country has the monopoly on goodness or badness.

And what about the violence? Jake seemed to be operating on an Old Testament level, an eye for an eye and all that. But what did I think about it? Was violence the only way of dealing with violence? I know I felt glad that Jake was going to give Shitface what for. I felt avenged, but in the long run what did it solve? He would probably do it again without a second thought, justified by the fact that he'd taken a beating. What sort of God was it that created a world where the animal who has the ability to rape is usually physically stronger than his victims. There's no balance there. Don't blame Me for that, God said. Mankind are free agents.

— ELEVEN —

DEIRDRE MANAGED TO avoid me for over two months all in all, not without help from Louie and Billy. It felt like a conspiracy. I could understand Billy's part in it, but Louie was different. I'd begun to think she liked me. Loyalty's a funny thing, powerful, indulgent and often stupid.

I saw Jake several times. He stayed over more than once but squarely refused to discuss what was happening to us beyond saying from time to time that perfect mashed potato didn't have lumps. I was supposed to be able to understand everything from that one enigmatic phrase. Tinker philosophy, I suppose. I did find out how the grapevine between him and Louie worked. Jake was resident watchdog at the house in Selly Oak. He sat on guard in case Deirdre or Louie needed him, particularly with clients who were new or they felt uncertain about. He got a cut too. I wondered how much they had to make so that all the hangers-on would be satisfied. Even Tom was on the books as ferryman and roving advertiser.

The night Deirdre had copped it Jake had been conducting business elsewhere, but the client was a regular so no one had suspected anything. He'd flipped, insisting that he didn't want to use a sheath. Deirdre had stood her ground but lost the battle. He'd had his way. He was subsequently punished in kind and promised to behave.

The gin and chocolates I'd seen at Deirdre's that day of revelations had been a present from him.

"It's sick," I said to Jake. "The whole thing is sick. He might do the same to some other woman."

"Naw," Jake replied. "He knows his balls are on the line."

"And that makes it all right?"

"It's the way things are, Bernie. You have to face facts or else run back to rural ignorance in Waterford."

Molloy had made his deal, much to Smith and Hawkins' disgust, but everyone knew that it was only a minor skirmish in a long-drawn-out war. They'd be back, but the next time they'd do it better. Ranks closed. Tom stopped allowing his taxi to be used to ferry stolen goods. Dan closed off the retail outlet in the pub. The battle was on.

In the end it was Billy's inability to hide his emotions for very long that helped me catch up with Deirdre. I caught her at the flat on one of her forays back for a chunk of undisturbed sleep. She looked awful and twice went to vomit while I was there. I told her the trade was making her old before her time and that she should pack it in. I made tea, the great healer, but she wasn't having any of it.

"Life is a mess, Bernie. It's not like the fairy tales old Isobel used to tell us. It's not God's kingdom on earth like Father Molloy insisted. It's a cesspit. You do what you have to do to keep from drowning in it. Now bugger off. I feel like shit. I want a bit of peace," she said as a sort of dismissal.

"Why did Man and Dad love you best?" I asked.

"Because they did," she snapped. "I've just tried to tell

you, life isn't fair. Go and read your effing books; maybe you'll find some answers in them."

Knowledge is power was one of the things I'd learnt from reading Tressel. I prayed for guidance. I admit I did it half-heartedly and that if God had a quarter of the wisdom He was supposed to have He would have dismissed my pleas as insincere. Still, the effort was there. No word came back.

About a month later, a month of slowness and routine, the shit began to hit the fan. Jake came in one night looking green around the gills. He had a quiet word with Dan, then Dan had a quiet word with me: "Get over to Louie's." Tom did the honours as usual, allowing me to drive now that I was competent. He waited outside the semi with the engine running. I took it as a bad omen.

Deirdre was in her usual bedroom looking as if she'd been dragged through a hedge backwards. She was crying softly while Louie mopped her forehead with a sponge. She didn't see me come into the room even when I stood directly in front of her. She was off somewhere else entirely. Louie pulled back the bedcovers. Deirdre's thighs were a mass of cuts and grazes; her wrists bore the same marks. I hadn't seen these signs before but instinctively knew that she'd tried to take her life. What I didn't know until Louie told me was why.

She was pregnant after the assault by the sheath-free customer. She'd got some form of drug from one of her other clients which he said might bring on a miscarriage. Instead it brought on a kind of madness in Deirdre which caused the self-mutilation. It had taken all Louie and Jake's strength to hold her and calm her down.

"What can I do?" I asked Louie, feeling totally inadequate.

"Nothing about this," she said, looking at Deirdre. "She'll have to go through with the birth now. It's too late to do anything else."

"Then what?"

"Then we become lucky. The father of this unfortunately conceived baby is childless. He's willing to buy the child from Deirdre, after the birth, as long as she agrees on paper to give up all claim to it. He's a legal man and knows what he's doing."

"What?" I said. In fact I think I said it about half a dozen times until Louie slapped me back to reality. "No, she can't sell the baby. I don't care if he is a legal man, that's certainly not legal. It's wrong. It's horrible."

"Save your disgust for another time, Bernie. The choices are limited. Can't you understand what she's going through? Would you want the baby of a man who'd raped you? Would you? Think of that lad who tried to rape you. Think of it, for Christ's sake, before you go letting your tongue run away with you."

I did think of it and something inside me seemed to shrivel up. It was a pain but wasn't a pain, it was a nightmare. Slowly I began to feel Deirdre's agony. Nine months of agony until birth with all its own pain would release her. I cried then and Louie held me.

But there was more to come. You see you never really reach the end. Things are not linear and conclusive. They are like jelly seething about in all directions, rarely settling anywhere while ever there's an opportunity for motion.

Deirdre had a favour to ask me. That was why I'd been summoned. She wanted me to take over her customers for the last few months of the pregnancy.

"NO!" I shouted. I think the noise might have woken the dead if there had been any nearby.

"But Bernie, I'll lose them if you don't stand in for me. It takes so long to build up a regular clientele, and Louie can't possibly cover for me."

I shouted "No" a few times for good measure then ran out of the house. Tom had the taxi door open before I reached it. He drove me back to the pub without saying a word. I stared unseeingly out of the window fighting down sobs that felt like they would choke me if I released them.

In bed I shook and shivered and cried and moaned. I couldn't stop even when Jake climbed in beside me and held me tight. He was still holding me when Dan came in at seven in the morning with a pot of tea and a telegram.

It said: "Isobel at death's door. Come home. Mam."

— TWELVE —

I WAS RUNNING away from a situation and I knew it. I was only glad that I had a valid reason. It helped me maintain some sense of dignity in the face of Deirdre's reproachful looks. She couldn't come, of course, but she wrote long letters for me to deliver. A pack of lies from beginning to end, but no one criticised her for being absent.

Dan loaned me the money to catch the overnight cattle boat from Holyhead and Jake borrowed Tom's car to drive me to the port. All in all, everyone mucked in.

I felt dreadful throughout. Sorry for myself and carrying on a continuous inner dialogue about the rights and wrongs of everything. Jake was kind but mostly silent on the drive. It was only as he made to leave that he started to speak.

"Perhaps, Bernie, you should seriously consider staying at home now. Your mam will be needing some help and you know now that things here are not like the end of the rainbow you'd imagined."

I knew there was genuine concern in his suggestion, but it still galled me. I knew there was a certain amount of truth in what he said too, but I wanted to carry through what I'd started. Otherwise I'd never know what I was capable of.

"Perhaps I'll come back too, soon, when I've made a bit more money. It's not the life for the likes of us. 'Tis the money that's driving everyone mad though, isn't it? You've heard them in the bar. How they'll be going back to Killarney or Limerick or Antrim or Sligo, but not yet, not till they've made the money. What's the matter with us? We can't seem to settle and we can't seem to return home. But, if we trusted each other, perhaps we could do it, get it together, maybe work the land a bit?"

I looked at his dark shiny eyes but could detect no mischief there. He was as serious as it was possible for him to be. Here was a Jake that scared me, because I wanted him too much.

"Work the land? You?" I said, partly to conceal my vulnerability. "Your groin couldn't stay quiet long enough to set a row of potatoes. No girl within a twenty-mile radius would be safe."

He stared at me with eyes dimmed and hurt. I felt myself leaning towards him and quickly pulled back.

"It's just the way I am, Bernie; it's natural for me. I can't help it, I just love women. I'm curious about nearly every one I meet. I think to myself, now what would it be like to sleep with her? But the feeling doesn't last. I mean, usually after a few times in bed I start getting restless again. It's the way I'm made, that's all. I've got to be free."

"It's the way you choose to be because you're terrified of getting close to anyone. They might hurt you, mightn't they? Or run away and leave you. Best not to let anybody under your skin," I said angrily.

"Maybe I could let you in," he said at last as he leant over to touch my cheek. "What do you say?"

I wanted to say, yes, let me in, but I couldn't. "I don't trust you, Jake Maloney, any more than I ever did," I said instead, "that's what I say. You never talk to me about things, and now here at the last minute before the boat goes you're sounding like we're engaged or something. How many other girls are you sharing a bed with these days? Apart from me and Deirdre, that is."

His face set hard for an instant, then he laughed as he guided me towards the gangplank.

"It was worth a try, sure it was, Bernie. You're a pain in the arse for so many people I thought I'd be doing them a favour."

That's when I knew that he had, in his way, been asking me to have him, to love him. People jostled me across the gangplank. My own fear of rejection had made me reject him. I felt empty. I looked for him from the deck but he was long gone.

I had no sleeper booked, so I spent the night in the lounge together with scores of other sleepy individuals. Some of them drank a lot; some of them nursed fractious children or elderly relatives; some of them sang to the accompaniment of the inevitable accordion. It all took my mind away from the problems in England and set them firmly towards home. Deirdre's letters nearly burnt a hole in my bag. I refused to be tempted to open them, but I wondered what she might have let me in for.

Uncle Liam met me in Dublin in his battered taxi. He had soda bread, hard-boiled eggs and lemonade. It wasn't the breakfast I would have chosen, but I ate it gratefully as we set off on the long journey home. I slept most of the way; Liam was never a great talker and all he'd say about Isobel was that she was in a very poor way. It was a fretful sleep, because Liam was an erratic driver, another one who'd passed no tests. He relied entirely on his brakes as if the gearbox didn't exist. I hated to think what would happen if the brakes failed. He also stopped at several shrines during the journey to say three Hail Marys for Isobel and clearly disapproved when I didn't join him. I was busy making my deal with God, which involved, among other things, a promise to do what Deirdre wanted me to if He would, in return, spare Isobel for a little while longer. I'd no idea what Liam would have made of that unholy pact if he'd heard it.

What had I got to lose after all? My virginity was already gone and my innocence was being assaulted on a daily basis. I might as well go the whole hog and do Deirdre a favour into the bargain. She needed me after all and, it's a wonderful thing to be needed. I shoved all thoughts of Jake far back out of the way.

I woke up finally about a mile from home. I recognised the landmarks easily and felt a slight giddiness, a thrill of quiet excitement to be back in a place so familiar. It made me strongly aware of how much of a stranger I still felt in England.

It seems that after all there is a comfort in knowing the every-blade-of-grass of a place: the smell of it; the pre-dictability of it; the security of it. And some would love the sense of being a fish in a small pond, familiar with all its companions. But as the taxi slowed for the final bend before the house, I knew, but didn't as yet understand, that the risks I was taking in England, the discomfort and changes I was experiencing, were right for me. It was true that I was something of a loose cannon, a misfit, a displaced person, yet the grappling with uncertainty was giving me a confidence I knew I would need in the harsh grown-up world.

My abandonment of God meant that there was only the one life to lead. Free of the superstitious claustrophobia of the Church, I might have a chance to excel at something or to love with a mighty passion. I would probably never really belong anywhere. Perhaps that was my fate after all. Isobel didn't know it but her love for me and her belief in my "sharp little brain" had helped to shake me free of Catholicism. Though I still expected thunderbolts from time to time.

They'll come when you least expect it, God sniggered. I blew a raspberry and made Liam jump.

The house was full of relatives and friends, and the huge wooden table was straining under its mounds of jacket spuds, boiled cabbage, boiled bacon and onions. The smell of the food knocked me for six and threw me back to childhood. I longed to see Isobel. I had to make the rounds first of uncles, aunts, cousins, but finally Mam led me through to Isobel's room.

There was the picture of the Virgin Mary on one wall and the Sacred Heart on another. A candle burnt in front of a small crucifix on her bedside table. I looked down at the emaciated figure buried under a mound of blankets and gasped. What had happened to that tall – almost six foot – woman with the knee-length copper hair and the wide, open face.

Isobel held a wrinkled bony hand out to me and I almost fell on top of her. I hugged her to me, ignoring Mam's warning to be careful She felt weightless, insubstantial, as if she had already taken herself off to another place. I found myself wondering for one mad moment whether her soul had taken up most of her body and had now departed. When I sat back to look at her face, Isobel was still there in the eyes – so like my own – that smiled back at me.

"Bernadette," Mam said softly, "that's enough for now. Come out into the kitchen and let her rest."

Isobel's voice was a croak when she spoke, but she made it clear that she wanted me to stay and that she wanted to be alone with me. Mam left us, but I could tell she did it grudgingly. One more nail in my coffin.

"I'm so delighted you've come," Isobel said. "I can go in peace now. They're all wanting me to hang on but, you know, it's for their sakes they want me to stay, not mine. I've had enough; it's time."

Her voice was weak but clear enough as she went on to tell me that my Grandfather Joseph had visited her the night before. She continued talking about the Rising, the Troubles, how she and other women had made collections; how the Black and Tans had used her and the other women as sandbags to fire over; and how Joseph had finally been shot down by the same thugs outside their house for being out after curfew.

"But of course," she finished, "he's been waiting for me to join him ever since."

Her eyelids drooped towards sleep after the exertion of her long speech. I sat on a while watching her laboured breathing, aware that my deal with God was not to be honoured. I knew she would be dead very soon.

"It's a form of cancer," Mam said later when the crowds in the house had thinned. Dad sat – silent as ever in my company – by the fire, occasionally adding more peat to the roaring blaze. Something made me think of burial sacrifices. I bided my time until the three of us were alone before asking the question I'd rehearsed so many times. "Neither of you ever loved me, did you?" It came out in a sort of rush. Mam folded her arms tightly across her chest like armour plating. Dad spat into the fire causing a sharp sizzle.

"Deirdre said in her letter you were whining over something like that," Mam said. "I've talked to your dad and neither of us know what to make of it. We've always done our best by you. Or are you saying we haven't?"

So it went on. Question followed by accusation. They formed a solid wall: one end silent, the other outraged. Dad went to bed without a word within ten minutes. Mam and I sat and stared at the fire. I forced myself to go close to her and try and get some physical warmth, but when my hand touched her arm she jumped as if she'd been scalded. Memories came flooding in of times in the past when she'd rejected my touch. When I started crying with my head on her knee, she stroked my hair, but I could sense it cost her a tremendous effort.

I lay in my old bed tossing and turning, trying to decide if there was any point in pursuing my questions when they met with such resistance. A short cry from Isobel's room brought me to my senses. Here I was feeling sorry for myself while she lay dying alone. I rushed in to find her sitting up in bed looking alert and radiant. Mam and Dad followed swiftly on my heels. We all stared at Isobel, and I wondered if God had changed His mind about the pact as she looked so incredibly well. She smiled at us all and when she spoke her voice sounded like a young girl's.

She turned to face us and said, "I just wanted to say goodbye to everyone." And she did. She said goodbye, closed her eyes and left us for good. Mam and Dad both put their arms around me then. For the first time I felt like I belonged to them. I was only sorry it had taken Isobel's death to do it, and I knew it would only be temporary. I swore silently on Isobel's memory that I would never have children unless I could love them wholeheartedly. Lots of oaths and principles you're lining up for yourself, God said. What about adding "The Eternal God is thy refuge" while you're at it? Go to the devil, I replied silently.

THIRTEEN

THE LAYING OUT was done and the wake was organised. I went off to see Breda while the preparations went on. The walk was refreshing, cold and icy. Only a week and a half until Christmas. Isobel had died within a day of her birth sixty-four years before. I was sure Breda would be expecting me, as news would have reached her about me being home. I stopped on the bridge over the river a few hundred yards from her parents' house and remembered the tinkers' dance. It seemed a hundred years had passed since then.

Breda was running down the path to meet me when I turned back towards her house. I could tell immediately by her funny gait that she must be at least six months pregnant. I hoped she was happy about it. When she got close I could see she was. We swept up to her house arm in arm, excited like children, gabbling like ducks. Mick was leaning on the doorway. He was much improved. Less like a boy, more a man.

"So what's the story?" he asked as I shook hands with him. I told Breda and Mick as much as I felt I could tell them without betraying anyone. Deirdre, that is. Breda sat wide-eyed when I explained about Jake and my lost innocence. Mick went off to see the animals.

"I'm sorry you missed the wedding, Bernie. I always thought you'd be my bridesmaid, but you understand it was all done with undue haste. Then Mam and Dad moved in with Aunt Madge and left us this old heap to run. Not the way I imagined it would be," Breda said.

"Is he good to you?"

"He is and delirious about the baby." She paused, wriggled her hands a bit, then looked me straight in the eye. "You've changed, Bernie," she said.

"How?" I asked, although I knew what she meant.

"Hard to pin it down, just something about you; a bit less certainty but a lot more determination, if you know what I mean. I don't think England would have suited me after all."

"It's a strange old place right enough," I said, "but it's exciting, Breda, and scarey. Sometimes I don't want to get out of bed for fear of what I might have to face that day. Anyway, sure sex isn't all it's cracked up to be, is it? What d'you say?"

She laughed and squeezed my hands. Tears collected in the corners of our eyes. Were we laughing away our worries about the future or crying for the childhood we had left behind? I couldn't decide.

So we chatted on, me following Breda about the various tasks she had to do to keep things ticking over: milking the cow; feeding the hens and collecting the eggs; baking soda bread; digging over a little patch of land by the house. I mucked in and we filled in some of the gaps that time apart had made. I knew that Breda's life was the one that I had left behind. It could have been mine. There was no judgement in that, Breda was content, but somehow I'd always known that I wouldn't have been. Even though I loved the hills, the fields, the curve and sweep of the river, I doubted that I could ever come back to stay.

"It would be a mistake," Breda said when I told her what I was thinking. "Mick's uncle did it. He'd held this dream of home so long that when he came back he was broken-hearted to find that he didn't fit in any more. He went back to London with his tail between his legs. No, you're gone now, Bernie. There's no turning back."

I felt the truth of it so keenly at that moment I had to walk off on my own. It was probably made worse by the loss of Isobel, but it was there and it really hurt, like a huge thorn in the foot or a wasp sting on the lip, throbbing and aching. I didn't know then that it would never entirely go away. I had made my choice to run to England, and now and for the rest of my life I would never really feel at home anywhere. Losing Isobel I had lost my centre.

I walked by the river, following its scalloped path till I reached the crossroads. The rush of the water muddied to walnut by the rain and cattle crossing suited my mood. I considered laying myself down on one of the large slab-like stones and offering myself up, a sacrifice.

Responsibility's an awful burden, but it follows if you run away from it. These were Isobel's words jangling round my brain. I smiled to myself at her boldness and her strong opinions. In the rush of the water I heard her laughter. I stayed by the river, under the bridge – near where, Isobel told me, Grandad Joseph used to poach salmon – for the next hour, until darkness had completely settled. I was reluctant to let go of Isobel but knew that in the end I had no choice. The best I could do was remember her stories, her fierceness, her love of life, and carry them with me. Don't forget her love of God, He said.

I promised Breda I'd see her again before I left and kept open the offer for her to come over, even if only for a visit. On my way back up through the village I was in a dream, so when Father Molloy stepped out in front of me I nearly knocked him down.

"Sorry about your grandmother, God rest her soul," he said. "I'm glad you finally made it home, as the poor woman was asking after you all the time." He started propelling me towards his house as if it was the most natural place for me to go. In fact it was a place we'd all avoided like the plague during childhood for fear of Molly Cahill's sharp tongue and heavy leather strap. I knew Molly had passed on, but I was shocked that my fear of it was still so strong.

"You'll be needing the name and address of a good friend of mine in Birmingham. Father Flynn will look after your spiritual needs while you're in his parish. I've already told him you'll be calling on him."

The web stretches wide. It just hadn't occurred to me to find a church since I'd been in England. It didn't seem appropriate and yet back at home it seemed the most natural thing in the world. For them, not for me. I went along, of course; no use starting a war if it can be avoided. Father Molloy's house was dark, as I'd known it would be. Everything seemed to be in various shades of brown and anything that could be polished shone brightly. Whoever had taken over from Molly Cahill was doing a grand job.

Any lingering fears disappeared as I watched Father

Molloy flapping around his desk looking for all the world like an elderly farmer rather than the representative of the Holy Trinity. I relaxed.

"I met a nephew of yours in Birmingham," I said.

"That demon," Father Molloy said, swinging round furiously. "What were you doing to come into contact with him, I wonder?" His marble eyes fixed me.

"He comes into the place I work to eat sometimes." It was only half a lie, but I wondered if the ceiling might crash on top of me any minute.

"Well keep away from him, Bernadette. He's been nothing but trouble since the day he was born."

He pressed the piece of paper he'd been scribbling on into my hand and ushered me to the door.

"I'll see you at confession in the morning then," he said as he closed the door.

I couldn't help smiling. I thought it must be a wonderful feeling to be so sure, so certain about everything. To have it all set down for you in black and white; no messy interpretations to be made; no contradictions to grapple with. Set in stone: the Ten Commandments; the Holy Trinity; the Virgin Mary. Neat. Something in me longed for that sort of unambiguous solution, but the rest of me struggled against it like a cat protecting her kittens.

The funeral was sombre, but the wake was a joyous affair. There was no keening or wailing for she had been ready to go, and no one who believed in heaven doubted her right to a place there. The old fellas, including Father Molloy, got well soaked. In increasingly slurred voices they began telling tales, each trying to outdo the one before. The only man in the room who remained sober was my dad. Ramrod stiff in his regular chair by the fire. The only time he came alive the whole evening was when the singing began. He had a marvellous voice, deep and powerful. I watched him and I desperately wanted to love him, but what I felt was awe and an amount of respect, for he'd always been a hardworking man and fair to Mam.

I caught Mam watching me as I watched him. She signalled for me to follow her into the main bedroom, which she shared with Dad. She was sitting on the bed when I got there, hands in her lap, looking like a child in prayer. She had several things spread out on the bed. I recognised some of Isobel's jewellery.

"Isobel wanted you to have these things, Bernadette." She hesitated for a moment then pulled a grubby envelope out of her skirt pocket. "And this," she said handing it to me. "It contains a letter she wrote some time ago, when you were a little girl." I turned the envelope over in my hands. "Bernadette," she went on, "I'd prefer if you never opened that letter, but I promised Isobel I would give it to you. If you can't promise to destroy it without reading it, then at least promise me you won't read it till you get back to England."

She was pleading with me and I hated to see her in such pain, but when I moved to comfort her she stood up abruptly. "Well?" she said.

"I'll leave it sealed for now," I said.

FOURTEEN

IT WAS AN awkward leavetaking. So much left unsaid, so much curiosity unsatisfied. I was as big a culprit as everyone else. Mam and Dad seemed like distant relatives rather than the parents I'd known all my life. Now that I'd flown the nest they made no effort at all to persuade me to stay. The only time they both really smiled at me was when I was getting into Liam's taxi for the journey back to Dublin. Mam stood there with her arm round Breda as if Breda were the daughter and I the friend.

By the time we reached Kilkenny I had control of my sniffles and Liam had run out of pleasantries. I began mentally preparing myself for my return to England and the pub, strange resting place that it was. The letter from Isobel gave off an almost visible heat as it nestled in my coat pocket. Desperate for information as I was, I knew I wouldn't open it until I was safe in my room in Birmingham.

There was no one to meet me at the station when I arrived back. I hadn't let them know when I'd be returning. The city was full of Christmas shoppers and for a change people were actually smiling at one another, practising I suppose for the onslaught of rarely seen relations.

It was about halfway through the lunchtime opening when I got to the pub. Dan gave me a wide smile and several of the regulars raised a cheer. I dumped everything in my bedroom and set to on the sandwich orders. Billy grunted every so often as he slouched about. I felt sure he must be aware of the pregnancy by now, unless he was choosing to ignore it in the same way as he had the prostitution. I did feel sorry for him because I knew he must be going through hell, but he was hard to sympathise with because he was so clearly enjoying his self-indulgent misery. Dan only spoke to him when absolutely necessary, but he wasn't unkind. All things considered, Billy was lucky to be working where he was. Another boss would have booted him out long ago.

Later Dan and I sat for a time over several pots of tea chattering about this and that. Getting settled with each other again. I even told him about the deal I'd made with God. He shook his head slowly.

"I'm glad God let you down, Bernie," he said. "No matter what your intentions, I'm sure you couldn't have coped with that life even for a short time. Anyway, Jake's found a girl to fill in for Deirdre." Dan saw my embarrassment. "He found her trying to sell herself on street corners in Sparkhill. She was ripe for exploitation by one of the pimps, so Jake whipped her off to see Louie."

"I suppose Louie's pimp won't exploit her then?" I chipped in.

"Yes he will, I know, but he is family to Louie, and that's not on the same level as some of those other bastards. Their girls have no life at all, no choice and often no home. You don't know the half, Bernie. I keep telling you, get yourself educated."

"Do you approve then?"

"It's not a question of approval, is it? It's a question of support and trying not to behave like God Almighty by telling other people what they should be doing with their lives. Louie's doing a grand job with young Nancy, that's the important thing."

I left it at that. One thing I did know was that I didn't know enough about any of it to argue the toss with Dan. It was time to open Isobel's letter.

The letter was dated 1938. It read:

> Dearest Bernadette,
>
> I am writing this now so that it is fresh in my memory you will be reading it because I have died before your 25th birthday when I would have tried to explain it all. You have been like a daughter to me as I have brought you up since almost the moment you were born now you have gone to live with your true mother at last which is where you should have been all along and I miss your love and energy about the place mammy had a terrible time carrying you, sickness fainting bad legs sometimes I thought she would never see it through I prayed constantly to the Virgin Mary. One day I know you will sense that things between you and your mammy and daddy are not as they should be God's will is sometimes hard to understand and mammy doesn't want to ever talk about it you see she was taken advantage of Bernadette by an Englishman who she worked for. Do you understand what I'm saying she met Patrick who was to become the daddy you know when she was well pregnant with you he loved her and stood by her. I must confess that at first I was cruel and let the shame it brought on the family

outweigh your mammy's pain I sent her to a convent shut her away tried to hide her sin the convent was for unmarried mothers Bernadette. Mammy cried and screamed for a week before we sent her off she tried to drown herself and worst of all the nuns were wicked and cruel to her and the other unfortunate girls they beat them and told them they had to suffer for their sins. Patrick worked for the nuns as a handyman he saw mammy's misery and grew to love her it was he that came to me and told me I should fetch her home for the love of God. That is what I did in her eighth month the delivery was awful you came out breached ripping half her insides apart it was all too much for her she couldn't bear to look at you. That is why I took you to live with me to relieve mammy's pain and atone for my sins in sending her away when she had needed me most I had denied her.

It was thought that she would never have another child but thanks be to God Deirdre arrived the carrying and delivery of her was as different again as it could have been from yours Deirdre was luckier than you in some ways mammy and daddy gave her the love they couldn't give you but dear, me and you had the best of times and I loved you more than I loved my own children. As I write this you are seven you have gone home. I will love you always. Try and forgive God for his complex ways and forgive mammy and daddy for theirs.

The Blessed Virgin be with you.

Isobel.

A terrible sadness rushed through me for the unwelcome entrance I'd made into this world. Why hadn't the house been strewn with flowers and food? Why hadn't I been the cause of swelling pride in Mam and Dad instead of a continual reminder of rape and pain? And there it was then, confirmation of my status as cuckoo in the nest. An explanation for the indifference of my parents.

"You're feeling good and truly sorry for yourself," Dan said when I spoke to him.

"And why shouldn't I?" I snapped back.

"Because it won't do you or anyone else any good, that's why. It's not in your true nature to look inwards. You're a fighter; you engage with the world. It'll only make you feel worse if you indulge it: that's what melancholy does. I've seen it in others."

"It's a piss-awful world all in all. I'm not surprised people get depressed," I said.

"There's many a child grown up without any love at all. Remember that."

"I suppose you've got a sob story to tell, have you? A bit of one-upmanship in the sorry-tales stakes eh?" Dan left the room then, not in a rush of anger but with a quiet determination not to rise to my bait. Of course, I wanted someone to scream and shout at. I wanted to break things, tear things, anything to get rid of of the awful gnawing feeling in my chest.

You're not really alone, God said at that point. Oh yes I am, I replied. I am everywhere, always, He continued.

You're not a God of warmth and love; you're a God of terror. You feed on insecurity, vulnerability, a need for simple explanations. Walk in fear of the Lord, that's what

Your disciples say. I can't be held responsible for what My followers say, He bit back. What are You responsible for then? I asked. No reply came back.

Maybe the grief of Isobel's death overcame me, or maybe I did feel sorry for myself, or maybe I needed a period of quiet contemplation. Whatever. I locked myself in my room for a week and slept most of the time. I only crept out for food and drink in the middle of the night when no one was around. After a few days Dan stuck a note under my door. It was a quote from a poem by Andrew Marvell:

> But at my back I always hear
> Time's wingèd chariot hurrying near . . .
> The grave's a fine and private place,
> But none, I think, do there embrace.

He knew how to hit the spot all right. I found I was smiling in spite of myself. But when I looked in the mirror I now saw a different face staring back at me. The face of a brutal Englishman. Accepting that part of myself was the hardest thing I'd ever had to do. If I could have cut it away, like an arm or a leg, I would have done. I guessed that somewhere he might still be alive, a happy family man who had never given a thought to the consequences of his act, who had maybe done the same thing to a dozen other women. I fantasised about finding all these half-sisters and brothers and turning up on his doorstep to demand retribution. But I really had no desire to meet him; living with him inside me was bad enough. Was that why Deirdre disliked me so much? Could she see him when she looked at me? And now was the dreadful circle turning again as she carried a baby conceived in the same way, hated in the same way?

Two days later I decided I had to rejoin the world. Christmas overshadowed everything. The irony of that celebrated birth was not lost on me as I made my way tentatively downstairs and back to other matters.

FIFTEEN

THE NOISE WAS coming from the bar. Surely it wasn't open. I longed for a window to peep through, a chance to prepare myself for who might be there. I stood outside the bar taking more deep breaths. Before I could reach out to push the door open, it swung back and Dan was there looking at me as if he'd seen a ghost. He let it swing shut behind him, cutting off the chatter and laughter. We stared at one another for a second or two until I found my voice.

"I'm all right now," I whispered.

"Thank God," Dan said, sweeping me up in his arms. He hugged me for a minute, then held me at arm's length. "You're sure?" I nodded. "Well then, that's the best Christmas present I've ever had." He nodded to the door. "Shall we go in?"

The bar tables had been pushed together to form a long eating surface. They were covered with different coloured cloths and piled high with food and drink. It looked a little like the Last Supper but with Nancy in the place of Jesus. On her left sat Louie, Deirdre, Tom and Billy. On her right was Jake, a place where Dan had obviously been sitting, and then a spare place, all set out but empty. Dan strolled me round to it as the conversation lulled. It was Nancy who broke the spell.

"God, Bernadette, aren't you thin now," she said with

surprise. Laughter followed swiftly as I sank gratefully into my chair. Apart from a few smiles, winks and nods, the party continued as before. I found I was ravenously hungry and was able to hide any lingering embarrassment by stuffing myself until my stomach ached.

We played musical chairs, blindman's buff and pass the parcel for Nancy's benefit, until it was time to clear up before the next round of eating. Jake squeezed my hand as we removed the remains of turkey, stuffing and vegetables. Deirdre and Louie gave me a quick hug as they carried in the trifle and cake. I began to feel human again.

We were in the middle of telling a chain story when there was a loud rapping at one of the bar windows. It had an angry resonance to it. Dan climbed on one of the bench seats and lifted the curtain a little. I caught a glimpse of a round face under a balding head. It was a middle-aged man I'd never seen before. Dan dropped the curtain and signalled to Louie.

"It's Philip," he said to her.

So that was the cousin. The generous pimp. Louie looked more than a little distressed by the interruption. Dan offered to go out with her, but she refused and indicated that he should keep an eye on Nancy. Jake picked up the thread of the chain story and tried to keep it going. We all joined in but everyone's ears were tuned in to the row that was taking place outside. Nancy was beginning to look worried, when Dan fortunately remembered the Christmas crackers and took her off in the back to find them.

Louie returned a minute or so later looking flushed and unhappy.

"He says we have to work," she said to Deirdre. "He's turned five customers away already and won't turn away any more."

"But it's Christmas Day," Billy whined, stating the obvious as usual.

"Want me to have a word with him?" Jake offered.

"Thanks, Jake, but there's no point. His mind's made up. He's got the car running out there waiting to take us and he's threatening to let Harry Stratton have us if we don't do as he tells us."

"Stratton?" Jake said sharply. "I didn't think he was into pimping."

"He is now," Louie replied. I'd seen Jake's eye twitch nervously at the mention of Stratton.

"Who's Harry Stratton?" I asked.

"Someone you don't ever want to meet," Jake said bitterly. "He takes pleasure in hurting people, especially women."

I stood on a bench and lifted the curtains to look out. Philip was tapping the steering wheel and watching the pub door. He crunched the gears into position as he saw the group come out. It was a large car. Expensive looking. And next to Philip sat an expensive-looking woman. Black hair, high cheekbones and a fur coat with a great big collar. Jewels glittered on her fingers as she patted her hair into place.

"Who's that?" I asked Tom, who'd come to stand beside me.

"His wife," Tom said with a snort.

"And she knows all about his business?"

"Where do you think the furs come from?" he replied.

"She doesn't care how it's made as long as it's rolling in. She's no better than Deirdre and Louie, except she gets higher pay for her services."

Nancy was exhausting. She had enough energy for four people. It was fun, but I was relieved when the phone rang at eleven asking Tom to bring her home. There was apparently a lull in business. I spoke to Louie and asked her to tell Deirdre to phone as soon as she could as I needed to talk.

"It's a busy period, Bernie," she said. "Might be after New Year before she gets a day off."

I knew I was getting the brush-off, but somehow it didn't anger me as much as it would have done before. There was a certain extra calmness within now that I knew who I was. I liked the feeling. I knew I'd get to see her, by hook or by crook. It didn't take imagination, just a strong will.

As we prepared for bed, Dan began telling me a little about his past. It seemed I would find out about him in bits and pieces, like working out a jigsaw. In his youth he'd apparently toyed with the Independent Labour Party, attracted by their enjoyment of the spiritual and sexual as much as their politics, and often wondered where his life would have taken him if he'd stuck with them. But he'd been dragged backwards and forwards between Ireland and England as a young man, following his dad who was an itinerant musician, and unable to commit himself to anything, including love affairs. His mother had settled in Dublin, refusing to keep uprooting herself, but Dan was expected to accompany his dad to "save him from himself", him being fond of the bottled kind of spirits.

Dan and I eventually fell into our beds absolutely done in. Tom was so far gone that he made a nest for himself in the corner of the snug. No one seemed to know what had happened to Billy. He'd slipped off at some point without bothering to say anything.

Tom felt so ill the next morning that he couldn't even help Dan and me clear up. Dan sent him off to his bed to sleep it off. Before he went up he tossed me the keys to the car.

"Treat it gently," he said.

I chattered to Dan in dribs and drabs throughout the morning. Even though I was still feeling fragile, the familiarity between us allowed for silences without any tension developing. At about eleven he poured strong tea slowly into our mugs, giving himself time and space before speaking. We weren't letting the Boxing Day boozers in until midday.

"You're a very bright young woman, Bernie," he said at last.

"I hope so," I replied, not knowing what else to say.

"Shouldn't you be thinking about a future for yourself? You're not planning on making barmaiding into a career, I hope." His eyes were gentle as he watched me over the rim of his mug. "Much as I appreciate your talent for it."

"I haven't thought about it."

"Well now's the time. Just because Deirdre's got herself into a pit she can see no way out of doesn't mean you have to."

"Trying to get rid of me are you?" I teased.

"Not at all. You'd be welcome back here any time, but there's a whole world out there just waiting to be explored. Don't you feel curiosity about it? Aren't you hungry to know things?"

"Barmaiding and cleaning are the only things I know, Dan. They're not going to get me far, are they? I might as well skivvy here as anywhere else." He waited, deliberately leaving a silence for me to examine what I'd said. "I'm scared," I continued. "Coming here and finding my feet was terrifying, and at least I had a bit of family and people from the same place as me. You must have felt the same when you came, surely?"

"I've been here a lot longer than you. I got used to it quick enough after one or two lots of fisticuffs. You've got to adapt a bit if you're to stay in a place. If you don't want any challenges, best to go back home."

"There's little enough for me there, anyhow. And now and then I get this feeling that I'm searching for something. I don't know what it is, but it's almost as if I can feel this small hand on my back pushing me gently forwards. I'm going to take it slowly, Dan – try and find out what I'm looking for. I don't want to make any quick decisions like I did when I came here."

We called it a day at this point, because Timothy O'Keefe and one or two other regulars were jumping up and down outside the bar window. Billy didn't turn up for the lunchtime session. I considered calling on him, but I was too tired after the Boxing Day bonhomie. He was a grown man after all.

My dreams were full of questions. The problem was that I kept finding answers I didn't want, like bloodstained clothes, injured animals, faceless people in crowded corridors. I kept missing trains until at last I decided to take a coach. Unfortunately the driver of the coach was a baby and couldn't reach the controls. I woke up in a real lather. No wonder.

Billy didn't arrive for the evening shift either, but Tom was in better shape so he stepped in to help. At ten Dan suggested I take Tom's car – which, incidentally, Dan owned – and do a check on Billy.

"You never know what the fool might do, and Deirdre's got enough on her plate as it is," he said.

Billy's flat was in darkness, but I still had a key. I let myself in quietly in case he was sleeping. The place was an absolute tip. The remains of food sat on every available surface in all the rooms, together with empty beer bottles and overflowing ashtrays. It looked like he'd been sleeping in both bedrooms and on the settee. I could picture him restlessly mooching from room to room trying to find peace where none was to be had.

He was in a bad way. We'd have to put our heads together and see what we could do for him, but short of convincing Deirdre to come home – which seemed a less likely prospect than ever – I couldn't come up with a good solution. Unless it was to send him back to his mother, Noleen, for a holiday. A few weeks with her and he'd probably come screaming back to Birmingham begging for his job back.

I did think about doing some cleaning up, but only for a second or two. I really had no desire to mother him or anyone else. It was quite enough trouble keeping myself in some sort of shape. I left a note for him saying Dan was asking after him and set off for Louie's to see if I could nab Deirdre.

I parked the car opposite the house and settled myself in the back seat for a while to see if I could work out the comings and goings. Nancy's room was in darkness, so she was probably fast asleep. I wondered if Jake was sitting on guard. I'd soon find out. Two men emerged from the house shortly after I arrived. They had their coat collars up and were clearly trying to avoid looking at one another. Thieves in the night. I felt like winding down the car window and yelling obscenities after them. Both probably going home to oblivious wives with nice clean homes. Neither of them looked short of a bob or two.

I waited a while, biding my time and looking for any sign of movement in the house. That's when I saw the figure creeping over the fence of the neighbouring back garden and crouching under the window of what I knew was the room Deirdre used. I fought my first urge, which was to shout at him to bugger off; after all, he could be a client. I knew they got their kicks in a variety of ways, many of which didn't include intercourse. Louie was a good storyteller, though I thought she embellished the facts. She must have done. But watching the crouching figure I began to wonder.

The side door opened before I could speculate any longer. Jake sauntered out with his arm round a young woman I'd never seen before. My stomach churned. The worm of jealousy feeding. I slid further down in the seat hoping he wouldn't notice the car. Stupid to have parked it so close. Unbelievably, the crouching figure tried to nip in the open door of the house before Jake closed it. In the light from the doorway I realised it was Billy. Jake grabbed him by the collar without loosening his grip on the woman. He looked out into the road and saw the car. I wanted the ground to open up and swallow me as I watched Jake marching over to the driver's seat. He was already speaking as he opened the door.

"Hey, Tom, shake a leg . . ." He stopped as soon as he saw me. It was too dark to see if he blushed, but I hope he did. He stammered something about Tom as he let his arm fall away from the woman. She looked puzzled. Billy snorted like a pig. I didn't know if he was crying or laughing. Someone had to take hold of the reins.

"I'm driving tonight," I said as I climbed over into the driver's seat with as much dignity as I could muster. "Shove Billy in the back. I'll drive him home."

Jake shoved Billy in the back all right but then climbed in beside him. The woman, left standing in the road, ran round the car and jumped in the front. We drove in silence, apart from Billy's strange whimperings. At the flat Jake marched him down the path, took his keys from him and almost carried him in, as Billy had begun to dig his heels in the ground. I sat looking straight ahead, fascinated by the blinking of a faulty lamppost in the distance. The woman fidgeted and eventually took a pack of Woodbines out of her bag and offered me one. I thanked her and lit up, knowing full well it would make me feel sicker than I already did. One day I would have to take up smoking seriously, not just when a crisis hit.

I watched her out of the corner of my eye as she lit her own cigarette. She looked about sixteen, which meant she was probably only thirteen or fourteen. Her face was thick with pancake but that was the only make-up she wore. She was pretty in a damaged sort of a way, though her lank, greasy hair stuck to her head like a skullcap. Her fingernails were bitten down as far as they would go and the sides of her fingers were red with sores where she'd chewed repeatedly at the flesh. There was a life story in there somewhere. I wanted to ask her about it, but I knew it would probably be the same as scores of other tales Louie and Deirdre had told me. Was this the unfortunate creature who was going to stand in for Deirdre?

"Will you drive us to the station?" Jake asked when he returned. He looked flushed. "I had to knock the poor sod out to calm him down," he said as an explanation. "This is June, by the way," he finished before slumping back on the seat.

At the station I kept the engine running, ready to roar off to some quiet spot and shout my head off at the night. Jake got out and ushered the protesting June towards the station entrance.

"Wait for me. Please. I'll only be a minute," he said.

I watched them arguing and knew I should drive away. It was obvious he was changing horses in mid-stream and she was the loser. Something held me there though. Perhaps a warm feeling low in the pit of my stomach as I watched his thighs pumping up and down as he ran back to me. We all fool ourselves some of the time, and I knew I needed love as much as the next person. The only question was, how would I recognise it when I saw it?

Jake slid into the seat beside me and gave me a quick kiss on the cheek.

"June is the sister of Janice who's standing in for Deirdre," he said in a rush.

"Younger sister, I hope," I snarled. "She's only a child."

"They grow up quick in Yorkshire."

"You would know all about that, I suppose."

"Ah well," he said slowly. "That's another fairy tale shattered on me."

"And what's that?"

"I always thought Sleeping Beauty woke up more beautiful, more radiant and more loving than ever."

"Are you claiming to be a prince all of a sudden?" I asked. My irritation at being at the mercy of emotions I couldn't seem to control was actually making me feel shy.

"I missed you," he said softly. "More than I expected to."

"Oh, I expect you kept yourself occupied," I replied.

"Will we ever crack it, Bernie?"

"What's that?"

"This thing between us that we do and don't want. Don't give me that surprised look. You know what I'm talking about."

And of course I did.

The weakness of the flesh will always be your downfall, God said. Funny how He always seemed to be around when the flesh was being weak.

SIXTEEN

JAKE AND I spent the best part of two days together, in between work at the pub which he happily joined in with as Billy was still hibernating. Dan, Jake and I hatched a plan to try and get Billy home to Noleen. This involved writing a pleading letter, supposedly from Billy, saying that he was dying for some of his mammy's soda bread and boiled bacon; that the climate in the city was having an awful effect on his complexion, something which Noleen valued highly, and turning his teeth green at the edges. We asked her to reply to the pub, as his flat was being fumigated because of an outbreak of lice. We had great fun doing it, convincing ourselves that it was in his best interests and that he would thank us in the end. We were pretty sure Noleen would demand that he come home immediately for remedial treatment and that we would find some way of getting him on the boat, even if it meant Tom's cousin in Wolverhampton having to come up with a harmless drug. Noleen wasn't short of a penny, having been quite well provided for by her three husbands. If nothing else it would give her something to gossip about for the next ten years.

Underneath all the fooling there was a real concern for Billy, who had gone from a likeable fool to a bit of a dribbling slob in a matter of months. I was confused as to how much blame could be laid at Deirdre's door, but Dan and Jake were adamant that he should have chucked it in with her long before.

Jake was called back for watchdog duty on the Tuesday. I drove him and insisted that Deirdre fit me in for a chat. Otherwise I would make a nuisance of myself in the street by following would-be clients and asking them awkward questions in a loud voice. Tom, who'd been standing in for Jake, took the car off but promised to call back for me before six.

Louie and Deirdre looked totally exhausted, like dish-cloths almost wrung dry. The strain of keeping Nancy occupied with either Dan or at other friends' houses and then trying to appear perfectly normal and alert when she returned was killing them. But Philip wasn't letting up. Louie said he'd called round at least twice a day to check on them and she was worried that something was brewing. Jake had heard some murmurings about fights between various pimps over territory. It seemed some new lads were muscling in on established patches. The way Jake spoke I sensed that things could get very nasty. As if they weren't already.

Deirdre and I sat in the debris of her room, enveloped in a mist of Evening in Paris. She seemed to tip a whole bottle of the damn stuff on the bedcovers whenever a client left.

"We just haven't the wherewithal to be able to change the fucking sheets after every one. It's a matter of swapping the top for the bottom and vice versa until it gets too much. I can't stand the smell of them. It's disgusting. Costs me a fortune in perfume."

I knew she was jabbering away in order to put off the moment of serious talk which she'd been avoiding for long enough. I let her go on for a while and watched the nervous way she moved and the tension in every line of her body. Her breasts were much larger than they had been and the mound of her stomach was rounder and firmer. What did it feel like, I kept thinking, to have another body growing inside you, living off you? What could it feel like when you had no desire for it to be there at all, but short of bumping yourself off there was nothing to be done? It would just grow and grow, totally oblivious. Would you hate it? Could you avoid despising the very air that it breathed? Or was it possible somehow to transcend all of that and maybe build a bridge towards this little creature that was struggling into life? There should be a way to stop these things before they got on to the road to becoming something; before they became more than a speck of flotsam drifting down the fallopian canal. Of course I was thinking of myself as much as the creature inside Deirdre.

"Does that bastard still come to you as a client?"

"He does, but he doesn't touch me now. He just sits and strokes my stomach and croons over the baby."

"How can you? How can you let him? It's so disgusting. It's worse than that; it's almost fucking evil."

Her stare seemed to go right through me. It was cold. It was closed off from me. There was no way to connect.

"Bernie!" she snapped. "You know what the trouble with you is? You think this fucking baby is *you*. You think if you can change my mind and get me to keep it, then somehow it will make up for Mam not wanting you. Well it won't. I didn't want the little bastard in the first place, and nothing, nothing you can say or do, will change my mind. I don't even want to look at the fucking thing when it's born. I don't even want to know if it's male or female, dead or alive. *Do you understand?*"

The doorbell rang suddenly, filling the room with its sickly chime. Deirdre's next client. Jake poked his head round the door. "Okay?" he asked Deirdre.

Okay? He must have heard us talking. How could he ask if things were okay?

Tom was late getting back, so I stood out in the street walking slowly up and down, up and down, keeping the chilly air at bay. It felt as if snow might be on the way. There they were, all the ordinary people in the street, tucked behind their curtains, safe behind their bricks and mortar. What made their brows furrow? A stain on the tablecloth? Dog shit in the garden? Tom screeched into the street as if the very devil were on his tail.

"Sorry, Bernie," he said. "I went over to roust out Billy, but the poor sod's not moving. There was nothing in the bloody place, so I hopped over to Maddy's store for tea and milk and such like. You okay?"

"Fine, Tom," I said. "Top of the world."

Jake came running out just as we were pulling away. He stuck his head in the window. Little boy lost expression. I knew just what was coming.

"I'll be tied up for a week or so. One or two things to sort out," he mumbled. I wound the window up without answering. Tom started whistling "Old Man River" to hide his embarrassment. As we turned the corner on to the main road, who should be walking up from the bus stop but June. I sighed. It seemed the only worthwhile thing to do at the time.

I was glad to be busy when I got back. Dan was giving me those "what the hell's up with you" looks. He'd had enough of my dramas. He deserved better treatment. Amazing where you can dredge up a smile from when you really try. It worked on Dan so I turned it on the bar. Timothy O'Keefe grinned back as he made strange gestures at the man standing beside him. I'd no idea what he was on about; the man was a stranger to me. All I could see was a full head of dark wavy hair. When the head turned towards me I was struck by the beauty of the man's face. Also, now that I could see it full view, there was something familiar there. He stretched his arm out over the bar to shake hands with me.

"Colm Connolly," he said. "You've barely changed at all."

— SEVENTEEN —

COLM CONNOLLY STAYED around for two days. He was on his way back home to tidy up his affairs before moving to England to work. We hit it off like nobody's business, spending hours reminiscing about the old days when we lived close by, gossiping about people we knew in common and generally gazing into each other's eyes. I was relaxed and happy about the situation. It was like a small still pool in the middle of a desert heaving with problems. I didn't expect anything lasting to come out of it and it didn't seem to matter at all, except for the worry that I might be doing it to get my own back on Jake. We made love once, and afterwards, as I lay in the curve of his arm, I felt more relaxed than I ever had done with Jake. Maybe it was the common history, maybe not. Maybe it was the fact that there was no sign of regret on Colm's face. Maybe it was wishful thinking, God chipped in. He couldn't seem to keep away.

During slack periods Colm would take Dan's piano accordion from behind the bar and blow up some tunes and songs. He always gazed at me when he sang the sloppy ones, and all the old buggers in the bar would nod their heads along with him and tap their toes to the rhythm. God, how they loved the sentimental stuff, and them tough as old carcasses when they were stone cold sober.

Dan told him he could come back any time and work in the bar. He'd been a great help with Billy still absent. Work had been a pleasure. When I saw him off at the station I had no regrets. He said he would be in touch when he returned, but I'd grown used to broken promises.

I still felt generally unsteady, my inner world lurching between anxiety and that new feeling of calmness. It was something to do with a certain lack of expectation, I suppose, a sort of morbid fear that the worst was bound to happen. I talked to Dan, of course. He repeated his own history about how he'd never really "belonged", always felt outside of things. The coming to England had somehow crystallised it for him. He would never really belong anywhere. He accepted it.

"Now, losing Kieron, having him, my only son, turn out to be a spineless arsehole, that really hurt. You see, I really wanted to make up with him for what I felt I'd lost. Maybe I gave him too much, turned away once too often when he was nasty to his mother. What the hell, I lost them both," Dan sighed.

"Why did she leave you?" I asked, while a part of me felt I already knew the answer.

"I played around once too often, Bernie. Rose had warned me, but I couldn't resist an attractive woman, had to play up to them, see if I could get a reaction. It was a challenge, I suppose. I needed them to want me. Needed some sort of continuing proof of my sexual attraction. Didn't matter that Rose loved me, found me sexually exciting. I'd won that one, needed new challenges. Didn't realise till months after she'd gone how much I'd lost. Too late. It's been ten years now and nobody's ever seen hide nor hair of her."

"There's been other women though."

"One or two."

I realised that he didn't want to pursue the matter of other women so I changed tack. "Am I a lost cause, d'you think, a misfit?" I asked.

He took my hand and squeezed it. I felt a surge of heat run up my backbone. "No more than any of the rest of us," he said. He continued to hold my hand for several seconds. I was truly disappointed when he let go and patted me like a favourite dog.

I didn't have the courage to initiate anything with Dan, though I was sorely tempted. It all seemed too murky to consider stepping in. Satan is tempting you, God said. He will always tempt you now that he's won you over a few times. Don't listen to him. I'm afraid Your side of the fence looks a bit dull, I said in reply. Where's the excitement in self-denial? Where's the dignity in losing your pride? He asked. Pride is a sin, I answered. Then there was silence.

Dan was biding his time, but I knew he'd start up again about "my future" before too long. He'd left details of correspondence courses in all sorts of subjects casually lying on the kitchen table. If he knew I had carnal longings for him, he hid the knowledge very well. And for me, I soon discovered that my intermittent lust for him was only a fantasy, something to toy with in quiet moments.

For the next month it seemed as if I was ticking over. I called at Billy's every so often to make sure he was still in the land of the living. I rarely saw Deirdre. It was almost unbearable watching her belly swell and seeing how much she hated every minute of it. I felt guilty about trying to persuade her to rethink her decision about selling the baby. It had taken an awful arrogance on my part to do that, and of course she'd been right when she'd said I was thinking of myself. Now when I saw her I thought of Mam with me growing inside her. There was so much of me that felt worthless I had no place telling Deirdre what she should do.

We'd had no word from Noleen about Billy, and Dan was beginning to despair. He was too kind a man to sack Billy, to kick him while he was down, but he couldn't keep supporting him either. Then one Monday evening Billy walked in looking a lot like his old self except for a fierceness in his eyes. He made no attempt to come behind the bar. He just perched himself on a stool close to the fire near Tom's corner. Dan waited ten minutes or so before he went over. The pub was still relatively empty.

"Well, Billy," he said, "you ready for starting work again?"

"I wouldn't work in this shithole again if you paid me a fortune," Billy replied. There was real malice in his voice. Dan took a step back, shocked by Billy's reaction. Tom came up to the bar and bought a pint for himself and Billy and nodded to Dan to leave it alone. We got busy soon after and both of us forgot about the silent duo, except to note that Billy was drinking heavily even by his own standards.

When Deirdre arrived with Jake at about ten, Tom was playing dominoes and Billy was staring sullenly into the fire. He didn't turn to look at Deirdre, but I could tell by the way his body stiffened that he knew she'd come in. Jake came up to the bar for the drinks. I'd barely seen

him since the night Colm Connolly had arrived. He still
had an effect on me, a flush up the back of my neck, a
thudding in the pit of my stomach, but I was determined
to stop the rot.

"I've missed you," he said as he took his change. I
knew he meant it. He meant it whoever he was saying it
to. "Can I stay tonight?" he asked when I didn't respond
to his first ploy.

I shook my head and, worried about my fragile determination, I walked to the end of the bar and over to the
fire. I was poking it quite forcefully, displacing my anger,
when Billy suddenly leapt up from the stool nearby.
He made a noise like an injured dog and headed straight
for Deirdre. His arm was raised above his head. I went
cold when I saw that he was holding a large crowbar.
Tom must have seen it at the same time as me. He jumped
up and threw himself between Billy and Deirdre. Jake
was pulling her down on to the floor under the tables.
Dan was running up from the other side of the room.
Everything except the arc of the crowbar felt too slow.

The thud and crack when the crowbar made contact
with Tom's head sent a swell of nausea round the whole
pub. Billy was raising the crowbar again. Dan was still
trying to reach him, but I was closer. I brought the heavy
poker down on the back of his neck with as much force
as I could manage. It slowed him up, set him staggering,
but it was the entrance of Smith and Hawkins at that
moment which finally stopped him in his tracks.
While they were grappling with Billy, Timothy O'Keefe
wrenched the poker out of my hand and kicked it under
the benches.

Dan was on the phone quick as a cheetah after food. Ambulance and Chief Inspector Molloy, in that order, I guessed. Billy was docile as Smith led him out. In fact I think he even giggled. Hawkins had his notebook in his hand, unable to disguise his pleasure at catching the Micks at it. He started ordering people around, herding them into different corners, and not once did he look down at Tom, unmoving on the floor. Someone put an overcoat on top of him. Dan checked his pulse. Still beating.

The ambulance and Molloy arrived together, which was just as well, because Hawkins had decided that none of us could accompany Tom to the hospital. We were material witnesses, he said. Molloy soon kicked the ground from under him. We followed the ambulance in Tom's car.

"Someone should go to the police station with Billy," Deirdre said in a choked up voice. I stopped the car. Nobody moved.

"Billy's too far gone to know what's happening to him," Jake said. Dan just grunted and kept his eyes on the road. Tom had been his friend for too many years.

Inevitably, at the hospital, we were shunted into a waiting-room full of injured people or their worried relatives. We stared at the floor; we walked up and down; we smoked fags; we were sick in the lavatories. Still no word about Tom. It was almost midnight when Louie burst in, clackety-clacking down the corridor in her heels.

"How is he?" she asked in a rush. "I can't stay long, I've left Nancy on her own. Will he be all right?"

We all shook our heads, feeling helpless surrounded by the monotony of the hospital routine. Louie joined our sorry band. By half past midnight Dan could stand it no longer. He marched into the forbidden area shouting Tom's name over and over again. He got an immediate response. A sister and a doctor accompanied him back to the public sector. Tom had been operated on and was now in a private ward. We could see him for just a few minutes and then we might as well go home, because there was no chance he'd regain consciousness before morning. Clear and concise, no questions please.

We were meekly following the sister to Tom's room when Philip suddenly appeared out of nowhere. He pulled Louie by the shoulder and pinned her up against the wall. Sister tried to intervene but, faced with Philip's raised fist, retreated and headed off, towards a phone I hoped. We were torn between going to see Tom and Louie's problem, but when Philip hit her a backhander across the head Dan flew at him. There was a slight scuffle before Dan and Jake frogmarched Philip out of the building.

Deirdre and Louie slumped on the corridor floor side by side and set up a chorus of "shit, shit, shit". Sister didn't like this display in her corridor one bit and threatened to have us all thrown out unless we behaved properly. We did.

Tom was unconscious. It was the first time I'd ever seen anybody in that state. It frightened me. He was making dreadful noises, somewhere between loud snores and gurgles. Drips and shiny equipment were all around the bed. There was nothing we could do, but we said hello to him just in case he could hear us.

I dropped Deirdre and Louie off at Selly Oak, where we hoped Philip wasn't waiting. At the last minute Jake decided to go with them "just in case". Before leaving the car he asked if he could see me "a bit later". I said no. Unfair of him to try and get me while I was low. Very unfair, I thought. It didn't occur to me till later that he might have wanted comforting.

Back at the pub the police were finished. Molloy sat waiting for us.

"Tell us the story, Dan," he said. Dan reached for the whisky bottle Molloy had on the table. I went to bed.

I couldn't sleep. I heard Molloy and Dan leave at about two in the morning, presumably to see what had happened to Billy. Why after all the years he'd been with Deirdre had Billy suddenly flipped? I fell asleep eventually at about five. Dan still hadn't returned. At seven I was up again and headed out to the hospital.

— EIGHTEEN —

M<small>Y HEAD WAS</small> full of slivers of glass as I rushed through the quiet streets. It was only minutes before the rush-hour traffic would be piling up. Names and images kept bumping off the windscreen, where the faulty wipers were doing a bad job with visibility. Why had Billy done it? Why had Tom taken the full force of the blow? Why hadn't any of us been quick enough off the mark to prevent the tragedy? Then, quietly sneaking in amongst all of these questions, why had Smith and Hawkins come in at that particular moment? I knew I had an imagination well laced with paranoia; who wouldn't have in my position? But when I really thought about it I realised we hadn't seen the pair of them for some time. Their usual pattern was to get Dan at the worst moments. That meant opening time or closing time. Certainly something had been responsible for pulling Billy out of his stupor. Was there a chance that Smith and Hawkins could have set the situation up?

My head was thumping by the time I parked the car. I made a mental note to get legal on it as soon as possible. Foolish to give the boys in blue such an easy catch. I was running up the steps to the hospital so fast, with my mind on a hundred things at once, that I didn't see Dan coming out. He was with a handsome young woman wearing a nurse's uniform.

"Bernie," he said softly, "this is Tom's cousin, Rita." I shook Rita's hand. It was trembling and damp from wiping away the tears that rippled down her face.

"How is he?" I asked Dan.

"He died half an hour since," Dan replied. His voice came from a long way back in his throat. Rita stopped trying to control her tears and gave full vent to her grief. I went hot, then cold, then hot again in quick succession. Dead. No other word had such a final ring to it. Kind, funny, helpful Tom who I'd rarely heard say a bad word about anyone. It was unbelievable.

The three of us sat in the car park for the best part of an hour variously crying and comforting one another. Rita told us bits of Tom's history in between her tears. It seems he'd been in England for nearly twenty years all told, working first in the pits in Yorkshire, then on building sites in the Midlands. I learned that his unwritten partnership with Dan had begun one night six years earlier. I also learned Tom's real name: Sean Grady, thirty-nine years old, mam and dad both deceased, two sisters in Limerick and a brother in Killarney.

"Is there anything I can help you with, Rita?" I asked. "Things that have to be done for the funeral maybe?"

Rita straightened. I could see the nurse in her come to the surface as she lit a second cigarette from the tip of the one she'd just finished.

"Would you come with me to his rooms, Bernie? He has a swine of a landlord who'll take possession of everything if we don't move it quick. He expects his rent to the end of the week even if someone passes away."

Dan dropped off at Louie's to break the news there.

Rita and I sped on to Sparkhill. Tom lived in the area
where most of the Asian immigrants had settled. It had
always seemed such an exuberant but easygoing district,
people doing as much of their living in the streets as the
weather permitted. Dan had told me stories about how
male Asians had had enormous difficulty finding places to
rent when they first came over and how Irish women had
been sympathetic, possibly because of their own experiences of prejudice. It seems that many attachments were
formed, and, when women from the homelands came to
join their men, they sometimes moved into a situation
where they shared a home and a husband with an Irish
woman. Ironically, according to Dan, the women often
got on very well together, so that they sometimes sent the
man packing and brought up their children communally.

The streets were run down but cheerful, even if the
houses were desperately overcrowded. From my experience of being an "alien" I could understand why immigrants
huddled together with people of their own kind. You
could feel very lonely and vulnerable in a land that wasn't
yours and where your difference stood out like a sore
thumb. Fortunately for me, my difference hadn't shown
until I'd opened my mouth.

Tom's room was a part of the attic. It was tiny, with
the single bed shoved under the sloping end of the roof.
There was a Baby Belling two-ringed stove on one wall
next to a badly chipped square porcelain sink. A small
Formica table with one chair completed the fittings. He
had his clothes in suitcases or hanging on the back of the
door where he'd hammered in some nails. The place was
very basic but he'd kept it clean. I let Rita take charge of

things and followed in her wake, asking her advice before packing anything. On the wooden box that was his bed-side table stood a photograph of Louie. She was holding Nancy in her arms. The child looked to be about two at the time. I held it up to Rita.

"His most prized possession, I think," she said. I must have looked puzzled. "He was in love with Louie for years," she went on, "but he always thought she was too good for him, and he couldn't have offered her the security she wanted for Nancy."

Tom and Louie. I let my mind wander around that one while I continued to pack. Tom playing watchdog at the house while Louie worked. Tom driving clients back and forth, maybe watching their smug grins in the car mirror. Tom playing with Nancy at Christmas, displaying more energy and enthusiasm than the rest of us. Tom playing dominoes with Louie in his favourite corner. Tom lying dying in hospital while Philip smacked Louie across the head to get her back to work.

I drove Rita back to her digs in Wolverhampton. She talked all the way about how she'd been thinking of going home because things weren't working out too well. About the affair she'd had with one of the married doctors and how he treated her like shit since he'd grown tired of her. It was all so desperate. And now Tom, the only member of her family in England, gone.

"Why does everyone think about going home when things go wrong? It's like it's some sort of Mecca or promised land. They were quick enough to leave," I said rather harshly. She didn't reply. "I'm sorry, Rita, that wasn't fair, just my internal dialogue busting out. I'll get thrown in an asylum one of these days."

"No, there's truth in what you say," she responded. "I suppose it's like the family: you always think you could run back to Mam and Dad if all else failed and they'd look after you. Of course you conveniently forget how possessive they were, or how they never really listened to you, or how they disapproved of your opinions. Tom always said it was the natural condition of the immigrant to yearn for what they'd left behind and view it all through rose-tinted spectacles."

"Did Tom ever talk about going back at all?"

"No," she said sadly. "Maybe he'd still be alive if he had. His family was always big with the IRA. He came over here after the 1932 elections when de Valera and Fianna Fáil had their big victory. My mam always hinted that he was one of the IRA prisoners they released at that time, but Tom would never confirm or deny it. In fact he didn't like to talk about politics at all if he could help it. Something had happened way back when and he never wanted to go home, even for a visit. I suppose we shall never know for sure now."

At Rita's place we unpacked Tom's sparse belongings. When I discovered she wasn't on duty again until the following night, I persuaded her to come back to the pub with me and promised I'd drive her home at closing time if she didn't want to stay over.

The pub was quiet and subdued. Many of the regulars wore black armbands as a mark of respect for Tom. There was no loud talking or noisy jokes. Several of the men went over to pay their respects to Rita when they learned who she was. She sat in Tom's corner with Dan and Timothy O'Keefe until Jake arrived.

I watched from a distance while he charmed Rita, con-centrating all his attention on it, pressing warmth and comfort on her and eventually putting his arm around her while they sang a medley of sad Irish songs together. I felt no jealousy; rather I marvelled at his skill and at his success in making the evening more than desperation and loss. In a way I suppose it was a kind of memorial to Tom.

When he came over and asked if they could sleep in my room, how could I refuse? He was offering her something she obviously wanted, something that I couldn't give her. Was he being exploitative? Probably, on some level, but I knew he wouldn't hurt her in the way that a night alone with her memories and her fears could. But I made him swear on oath that he would make no promises to her that he couldn't keep. He agreed. Was I a fool? Was I seeing only what I wanted to see, feeling only what I wanted to feel? Did it really matter, in the scale of things, what I was thinking?

Molloy came in at closing time. He and Dan took a bottle over to their favourite table. After I'd finished clearing up I made to leave. Had to dig out some bedding for my night in the snug. Molloy called me back.

"Will you contact Deirdre for me?" he said. I knew and he knew that he knew exactly where to contact her if he wanted to.

"Your man Billy has gone completely over the edge. The doctor said he needs to be incarcerated until the hearing." He scribbled something down on a bit of paper and hand-ed it to me. "This is where she can visit him if she's a mind to, though I doubt very much he'll know who she is."

I started to leave again but Dan pulled a stool out and nodded for me to sit down. He offered me a Woodbine. I took it, thinking I might as well get the habit underway immediately as there were bound to be other crises shortly. Like, what the hell was going to happen to Billy?

"Molloy says Billy was muttering something about a reward and that he mentioned Hawkins' name several times before he was put to sleep. Ring any bells with you?" Dan asked.

I told Dan and Molloy the thoughts I'd been having about Billy. "As far as I can see," I said, "the only thing that Hawkins could have put up as a reward which would have attracted Billy's full attention is Deirdre." Molloy and Dan nodded. "So the deal must have been for Billy to create aggravation here or something like that and Hawkins would close down Louie's operation. Does that sound likely?"

"I wouldn't put anything past Hawkins," Molloy said, "but a fight in here? What's that going to achieve? A killing, now that's more like it. Dan's going to have a hell of a time with his licence over this. But I can't believe that Billy would go that far. He'd never have killed Deirdre or Tom intentionally."

In my makeshift bed in the snug a little while later, I could hear the soft drone of Dan and Molloy continuing their speculation. I threw all the ingredients into the pot as well and tried to find an answer. I fell asleep thinking about it and woke up in the middle of a dream which was a re-enactment of the event. I realised as I sat up panting in the dark that Billy had been lunging for Jake, not Deirdre, and that the noise he'd made had been a strangled version of "Maloney". We'd all assumed Deirdre was the target, but we'd been wrong. So that left the question: what had Hawkins told Billy about Jake that would make him murderous?

NINETEEN

D AN WOKE ME with a cup of tea at eight. He looked older than he had the day before. His eyes were ringed with shadows. I told him about the conclusions I'd drawn from the dream, and after concentrating on the scene in his mind's eye for a minute or two, he nodded his agreement. His shoulders sagged as he walked to the door. More problems, they seemed to say.

"By the way," he said before he left, "Jake has known Rita for some time."

Jake and Rita had, in fact, been the last thing on my mind, but Dan's words focused me on that emotional swamp. How little I actually knew about Jake after all. How little I knew about anybody when it came down to it, including myself. It was difficult to accept, but I knew there was something missing in me. I couldn't seem to feel things as much as others. Tom was dead, Billy and Deirdre in dire straits, and here was I coldly calculating the details of the events, such as what Smith and Hawkins had to do with it.

As I expected, Jake and Rita were gone when I went up for breakfast. Dan handed me a letter as I poured more tea. It was from Noleen, her reply to our communication. It added another layer of awfulness to the events. I couldn't bear to read it. It lay there in my hand like a cockroach. Unwanted. Unpleasant. Dan took it back off me and tore it into little pieces. We finished breakfast in silence.

I phoned Deirdre and passed on Molloy's message. She was cold and distant. I could hear Louie crying in the background. I suggested clearing the flat up and she agreed to meet me there. After two hours cleaning the pub, the cellar, the kitchen and my room, I felt in better shape. Isobel used to say that the human body was like an engine which needed to be worked hard to operate efficiently. If it was left idle the battery went flat. Dan was like a tractor: solid, good over difficult terrain, easy to maintain. At the moment I felt like a finely tuned aeroplane: revving to the point of destruction and ready to fly off at a second's notice.

Deirdre had arrived early, avoiding contact with me as much as possible. She had most of her things packed when I arrived.

"What shall we do about Billy's stuff?" I asked.

"Leave it," she replied. "I couldn't bear to touch it. Except this." She held up an envelope which was stuffed with five-pound notes. "Now where do you suppose he got this from?" she asked. The question was mostly directed at herself, not me, so I kept quiet. I knew Deirdre had no interest in my theories.

"How are you doing?" I asked.

"Like shit," she replied. "What else? I'd give anything for a week's peace away from everything and everybody."

"Well then, why not use the money to go home for a rest?"

Deirdre slumped down on the bed and picked at the bedcovers with jabbing movements.

"Is that your solution to everything?" she said. "I didn't

see you staying there very long on your last visit."

"It's different for you," I said. "They both love you. They'd be delighted to have you home."

She looked down at her belly with disgust. "In this state? You'd have me go home like this!" she snapped. Before I could stop her she started thumping her belly and banging her head on the bedpost. I took hold of her hands and held them tight. She screamed and fought me until she was too weary to do anything but cry. Eventually she stopped sobbing and began talking. She was full of self-hatred to begin with.

"I'm such a mess, such a failure. You're right to be disgusted. I'm disgusted at what I let these men do to me. I'm disgusted at who I've turned out to be. And now that this . . . this thing is sharing my body. I just feel helpless, as if I'm being taken over."

I made some sort of inadequate comforting noises, saying something like "I know, I know" and that was sufficient for Deirdre to turn her anger on to me.

"You don't know! You'll never know. You pretend to be bothered but you're not. You're cold, Bernie. Cold like stone after a hard frost." I didn't argue. She was only putting into words things I'd already thought.

"After the baby, when it's all over, will you give it up, go and get a proper job?" I asked tentatively.

"What, work my guts out on an assembly line for a pittance and put up with the pawing of the foreman for nothing? What d'you think?" she spat at me. "I didn't rush straight into whoring when I came here, y'know; I did try 'proper' jobs. If it wasn't someone touching me up, it was someone telling me I was a 'thick Mick'.

Bollocks to that. There's a lot more money t'be made on
the game. Men will always be slaves to their dangly bits.
You bugger off and be 'proper' if you want to, see how
far it gets you."

She stopped suddenly and stared over my shoulder.
Hawkins and Smith were standing in the bedroom doorway watching us.

"Touching scene, isn't it, Smith?" Hawkins said. "A
couple of Irish whores telling one another some home
truths." Hawkins was red-faced but lardy around his
mouth and nose. He reminded me of bacon cooked in a
frying-pan on a low heat, tough but half-baked.

I began to get up, wanting nothing else than to smash
him in the face. Deirdre grabbed my arm and kept me
seated. Suddenly we were united against a common
enemy and we were very vulnerable.

"I'll take the envelope," Hawkins said, holding his
hand out. Deirdre ignored him. "Don't waste any more of
my time . . . I've got places to go." Smith took a few steps
towards the bed. A quick look passed between him and
Deirdre. A struggle for power. She needed to win a battle,
but I knew this wasn't the time or place.

I pulled the envelope out of her hand and threw it on
the floor. Hawkins rushed forward. His arm was raised
ready to hit me but Smith held him back. "That's not
necessary," he said quietly. Hawkins was livid. Smith
picked up the money and as he started to count it Deirdre
got to her feet.

"Let's go," she whispered. But they hadn't finished. They
stood blocking the exit. I saw Mr Singh from the upstairs
flat come into the room behind them. He exited sharply,

obviously familiar with the workings of the law in the area.

"Why don't you lot just pack up all your trash and get the boat back to the bogs, eh?" Hawkins said. Smith sighed as if in irritation.

"Excuse my colleague," Smith said. "He's not renowned for his subtlety."

Deirdre and I had gone into our say-nothing mode, but we held hands and I could feel the heat of our anger in that grip. Mr Singh saved the day after all. He suddenly appeared again, but this time he had three young Sikh men with him. They made a lot of noise coming into the room and greeting us like old friends. Unity is strength.

Smith shrugged his shoulders as he left with his pal in tow. "Dirt sticks together," Hawkins said as a parting shot. What had happened to him to make him so bitter?

Deirdre and I sagged together on to the bed. Mr Singh was talking ten to the dozen and gesticulating wildly, but he was speaking in Punjabi, which neither of us understood. One of the young men translated. The gist of it was that Hawkins and Smith had been visiting Billy on and off for over a week. He'd heard Billy arguing with them and seen them pushing him around. Then a few days previously it had all changed; it was as if Billy was an old pal of theirs. He even insulted Mr Singh in front of them, something he'd never done before.

We explained that Billy was in hospital and we didn't know when he'd be back. Mr Singh said he'd keep an eye on the flat and let the landlord know the situation when he called for his rent on the Friday. Deirdre pulled a couple of fivers from her pocket and asked Mr Singh to pay the landlord. He agreed.

Outside the flat there was no sign of Hawkins and his sidekick, so we loaded up Deirdre's things and I drove her to Louie's. She handed me a fiver before I left. "Only managed to get a few out of the envelope," she said. "Take it for petrol. Now bugger off and leave me alone."

I put the wheels in motion for a provisional driving licence that afternoon and also for a driving test. I was frightened about the extent of Hawkins' power and terrified of what he and Smith could do to me in the secrecy of a police cell. I wondered again why they hated us so much, but I knew I had to accept it as a fact of life. They did and they had power and resources and they'd roped Billy into their schemes, whatever they were. I spent a few minutes worrying about Jake, who seemed to be their prime target if my calculations were right. I got an image of him in Rita's arms, so I turned my attention elsewhere. Ah, so you do feel something, an inner voice said. I didn't recognise it so I decided to ignore it.

—TWENTY—

LOUIE INSISTED ON taking charge of Tom's funeral. She said he'd talked to her about dying and had wanted to be cremated. No one argued. It was clear that everyone except me had been well aware of Tom's feelings for Louie. We left her to it and on the Friday were informed that we could visit Tom in the chapel of rest. I ended up going alone in between the lunchtime and evening shift at the pub.

The place was polished and clinical. They even had plastic flowers in the urns placed around the reception area. There was organ music playing constantly: slow, morbid, unfeeling tunes full of gloom. I was shown to a small side room and left alone. The room was about ten feet by twelve, walls painted in institutional cream and green, tiled floor. In the middle of the floor sat the open coffin on a pedestal. It was Tom's body, all right, but something was missing: his spirit, or soul, or whatever you want to call it. I saw the body for the first time as it really was, merely a vehicle for carrying the individual human spirit around. I touched his face. It felt like cold, melted candle wax. Tom had gone; there was no point talking to his shell. I kissed him on the cool cheek and left, wondering if somewhere he was aware of my movements.

Molloy was waiting in the reception when I got there. He looked sick, as if the nearness of death made him fearfully aware of his own mortality.

"Dan said I'd find you here," he said wearily. "Come for a drink while you give me the details of your confrontation with Hawkins and Smith."

He took me to a café in King's Heath. Posh but plastic. I told him what he wanted to know. It didn't take very long and I was gnashing my teeth by the time I'd finished.

"I'm being leant on by the powers that be," he said. "Hawkins and Smith have obviously got someone's ear further up the hierarchy. I'll have to steer clear of the pub for a bit while they keep tabs on me."

"Bastards," I said with some feeling.

"Men like Smith and Hawkins are a special breed and, though they're attracted to the occupation because of its power, they don't all get in by any means." He paused, a faraway look in his eyes. "Pity they took the money, though. I'd like to have had a close look at it."

I handed him the fiver Deirdre had given me. He asked no questions but gave me five one-pound notes in return. It was the first time he'd smiled all evening.

"Does it worry you, death?" I asked him then.

"In what sense do you mean?" he responded. "If you refer to my own mortality, then no, I've long been aware of that. When my number's up I'll go quietly."

"It frightens me," I admitted. "The way one day you can be laughing with someone, looking into their bright clear eyes, maybe noticing a line on their face you'd never seen before, then the next day they've gone. For ever. No going back. No chance for things unsaid, for things undone. I never really got to know Tom, what made him tick, what made him happy or sad."

"You got to know some of it," Molloy said. "We only ever get to understand a part of a few people. Life's too short and we're too restrained to be able to do anything else. And you got to know Tom as much as most, so Dan tells me."

A large sigh crept up from my toes and sent a shudder through me. I was shocked to realise that my bravado was under threat.

"Death should be shocking," Molloy said. "We need to be reminded how little time we've got. It's just, well, in my job it's difficult to keep in touch with humanity. I spend a great part of my life face to face with the murkier side of things. Satan's territory, my uncle calls it. That's the way of it."

"And what about God's territory?" I asked, curious to know what a nephew of Father Molloy would make of that.

"God is it?" he laughed. "Ah well, now he abandoned me a long way back. I was told I had to trust in him so I did, and he never showed up when he was needed. Either he's got a wicked, cruel sense of humour or I'm not on his list. One way or the other, I won't be hanging about for him to show himself. Now Satan, him I've met and I wouldn't for one moment underestimate what he's capable of."

Was it my imagination or did the sky go dark for an instant? The lights in the café certainly flickered, and as I glanced around everyone seemed to be looking in our direction.

"Tell me about yourself," I said suddenly.

"Bernie, look, it doesn't happen like that." Molloy took a deep breath. "You need to take it one step at a time. There's a sort of hunger in you for knowing, but believe me that's a rare thing. The usual is to not want to know; to cut the easiest path through the forest. You'll always have difficulties, because you expect so much."

"How can you know all this about me when I know so little about you? And don't say it's because you're a policeman."

"But that's partly why, and it's also because I talk to Dan who worries about you a lot . . . Bernie, be a little kinder to yourself. Since you came over here you've had to become, I don't know, older . . . much older than your years."

The waitress began hovering near our table. Time to order more food or vacate the place in favour of paying customers.

"I'd better get moving," Molloy said. His eyes seemed to look right into me. I quickly put the shutters across the most vulnerable places.

"Yes . . . back to the spit and sawdust," I joked, and we became semi-strangers once more.

In the car-park he nodded towards Tom's car.

"If you need a few lessons before you take your test, let me know," he said with a smile.

The funeral took place the following day. Most of the regulars from the pub were there, together with Louie, Nancy, Deirdre, Jake, Rita, Dan and myself. A crowd of about twenty-five all told. A good job too, because the chapel was large and bare and unfriendly. I thought of Isobel's funeral and wake, which had seemed like a party in comparison. The coffin was at the front in the centre of a sort of stage. Behind it was a pair of purpose-built

curtains which I knew would open when the time came
to toss Tom to the furnace. The thought set me shivering.
Dan took hold of my hand and squeezed it.

Jake walked to the front of the room. He was carrying
a dog-eared book. I recognised it as the one that Tom had
often carried with him. Poetry I'd thought. I'd never seen
Jake look so sweet and innocent. He was wearing a dark
suit, white shirt and dark tie. Only the dirty brown
brogues on his feet hinted at the usual sloppiness of his
dress. He coughed a couple of times before he began to
read from the book.

"There's a lock in my heart, which is filled with love for
you, and melancholy beneath it as black as the sloes. If
anything happens to me and death overthrows me, I shall
become a wind-gust down on the meadows before you. I
am stretched on your grave and you will find me there
always . . . There is the cold smell of clay on me, the tan
of the sun and the wind . . ."

The reading lasted about ten minutes, and as he finished
Rita moved to stand beside him and one by one we went
up to pay our last respects, men and women shedding
equal amounts of tears. As Dan and I walked up, the
curtains opened prematurely and were swiftly closed
again. Dan laughed. It sounded like a gas explosion in
that barren place.

"That's Tom all right," he said. "Always ahead of himself."

With that the mood of the mourners changed. We left
the chapel as the curtains opened once more, no one
wishing to stay to watch the coffin slide down the runway.
At the pub the singing, drinking and toasting began.
Memories of Tom were shared as his spirit was sent on its

way in the traditional manner he would have appreciated.
A horn blasted outside the bar window at one o'clock.
Deirdre and Louie left hurriedly. Philip, I presumed. The
man was becoming a menace. Jake watched them go, his
head on Rita's shoulder. He'd been sacked as watchdog
since the confrontation with Philip at the hospital, but I
knew he worried, as we all did, when Deirdre and Louie
were alone with their clients. Nancy spent the night at the
pub, the following day, Sunday, being her day with
Grandad anyway.

I caught Jake alone in the passageway to the toilets
before he and Rita left. He was a bit worse for drink but
fairly coherent all the same.

"Have Hawkins and Smith any reason to want you out
of the way?" I asked him.

"They don't need a reason," he said.

"I know, but have they one?"

"More than one. Easily more than one." He inclined
his head towards the bar. "I'll be back to see you later and
we'll talk about it more."

"No, Jake," I said firmly. "Talk to Molloy. It's him needs
to know."

On Sunday I forced myself to go and see Billy. I wished
I hadn't. He was so far gone that he didn't recognise me.
He talked as if he thought he was back in school in
Ireland and the headmistress had caught him out in some
misdemeanour. That was his explanation for why he was
locked up.

"I can't get any sweeties either until my mammy comes
and sorts it all out for me. Have you seen her today at
all?" He said it all in the sort of sing-song voice that

young children often use. I tried to get him to talk about Jake and Tom, but all I got was a blank look. Only Deirdre's name raised a reaction.

"She's a very naughty girl," he said peevishly. "But she'll be punished too when Mammy gets here, you wait and see."

He was concentrating hard on picking a scab off the back of his hand when I left. I knew that we should contact Noleen and let her know what was happening, but I was honestly scared to death about how she would react. She'd never been out of Ireland. As far as I was aware the furthest from home she'd ever been in her life was Cork and that had been a trip organised by Molly Cahill. She may have buried three husbands, but that was chicken-feed compared to what she would have to go through if she came to rescue Billy. And I was no longer certain that it was possible to rescue him.

TWENTY-ONE

NOLEEN DID COME over for Billy's trial. She was a grey imitation of her former self, meek, frightened and almost speechless. She stayed with Rita, went to mass as often as she could and made the sign of the cross every time she left the house. As far as she was concerned, the land of the heathens was responsible for what had happened to Billy and we were all conspirators in his downfall. The priest – Father Molloy's pal – told her that none of us had ever attended church while in his parish, and that confirmed all her worst fears. We were lost to God and therefore abandoned by him. Everything she said was spoken in a hushed whisper as if she feared God might strike her down for even being in our company. I began to wonder if He might myself, but as He hadn't deigned to speak to me recently I put the matter to the back of my mind. I had begun to notice, however, that He was often missing at the most crucial moments. Times when succour in great measure was required. If questioned about these absences His most frequent excuse was the activity of Satan. Must be useful to have a fall guy, 'scuse the pun, a bit like Jekyll and Hyde. One side is good, the other is bad. Very straightforward and very unlike life itself.

Deirdre kept well out of the way. Everyone was sworn to secrecy about her whereabouts and her condition. Neither she nor I attended the first days of the trial, but

Jake gave regular reports in the pub. Billy's legal representative was pleading insanity and Billy's presence in the court more than verified the claim. Jake said he was like a little boy on stage in his first acting role, rarely speaking, but when he did fluffing his lines. However, when Hawkins and Smith gave evidence, Jake said Billy had to be taken out of the court because he started shouting at them calling them "the Devil's own messengers". Deirdre and I gave evidence on the same day. Molloy had told me there was no point in airing my views about Billy and Jake as it would make no difference to the outcome of the trial and would only set Hawkins and Smith on the defence and consequently on my tail.

Rita did her best to keep Noleen out of the courtroom on that day but she failed, and when Noleen saw Deirdre she got down on her knees in the middle of the aisle and started saying the rosary. It was dreadful. She was threatened with contempt of court and had to be led out by Rita and Jake. Any more revelations and I think she would have collapsed from nervous exhaustion. Deirdre had no sympathy to spare.

"Senile old biddy," she said. "They should lock her up with her mad son." I nearly slapped her then. It was only the thought of the baby that stopped me.

Billy was found guilty of manslaughter but with diminished responsibility. His lawyer asked that he serve his sentence in a psychiatric institution. The judge agreed, but added that he should be confined indefinitely. Noleen screamed when the judge had finished speaking, and Jake said he could hear Billy shouting for his mammy as he was led away.

Noleen had the biggest decision of her life to make then. Would she go back home or make a life in England so that she could be close to her only son? Her son who would probably not know who she was even if she visited him as often as permitted. As luck would have it, Rita was made a Sister that very week. Her new duties at the hospital were arduous and she couldn't get time off for over a month. Someone had to take Noleen home. She was quite incapable of travelling alone. She said she would make a decision about her life after consultation with Father Molloy. It was Wednesday. On Thursday lunchtime Jake came in. He was pale and tired-looking.

"There's trouble," he said to Dan.

"How's that?" Dan asked.

"I've just heard that Philip has agreed to sell Louie and Deirdre to Harry Stratton. He's been spreading his wings for some time now, moving his drugs and gambling into the pimp business. He's ruthless, Dan, y'know that. Nobody crosses him. I've heard he has seven or eight girls to a house with a minder and twenty-four hour service. He's said to be a real sadist himself and encourages the worst possible sort of client. Some of his girls have been hooked on drugs and ended up in ditches."

Dan and I were both speechless. He found his voice first.

"Philip can't do that! The girls won't stand for it. There's Nancy to consider. I mean, he's her fucking uncle of sorts."

"Louie and Deirdre won't have a choice," Jake said grimly. "If Philip has done the deal, then they're Stratton's property now and he won't take any lip. In some of his houses he's got girls not much older than Nancy available for clients. This is serious, Dan. Deadly serious."

Dan was out from behind the bar in a flash.

"Stay here and help Bernie," he ordered Jake.

"Let me go with you," I said, following him to the door.

"Two's a crowd," he said as he shut it in my face. The clock seemed to crawl around to closing time no matter how hard I willed it to move. Jake was more distracted than I'd ever seen him. Dan phoned at three.

"Get round here to Louie's in Tom's car right now and bring Jake with you," he said before slamming the phone down.

I could feel disaster overtaking us as I drove. Jake was as worried as me and that didn't improve my mood. Coming up against someone like Stratton was no joke. My legs were like custard when we pulled up outside Louie's. All the lights in the house were blazing. The curtains were closed. Philip's car was parked in the drive.

I knew Dan must have lost his mind, when I walked into the living room. Philip and his wife were tied to hard-backed chairs with an assortment of belts and ropes. They had handkerchief gags in their mouths.

"Oh no," Jake said. I knew he was thinking what I was thinking. Timothy O'Keefe was with Dan. He looked as if he'd already been sick a few times. Deirdre, Louie and Nancy were sitting on the settee. They had their coats on and suitcases by their feet.

"Right," Dan said. "Get them out of here." There was no arguing with him, and I knew that every minute I spent in the house brought me closer to Harry Stratton. Jake helped us load up then went back into the house.

"Where to?" I asked.

"Dan's," Louie said.

"Billy's," Deirdre said.

As I hit the Pershore Road they'd decided Billy's was the best bet. Nancy looked like she'd been hit by a sledgehammer. I wondered what she was making of it all.

"Why did Grandpa tie Philip and Janice up?" she piped up when I stopped at the traffic lights.

Louie kissed her on the cheek and managed a smile which didn't reach her eyes.

"Dan's just playing a little game with them, sweetheart. He went to see one of those gangster films he likes and now he's showing Philip and Janice what happened in the film."

I gave Louie top marks for invention, then thought about it. Of course! Dan was doing what his hero Robert Mitchum would do in similar circumstances. The problem was that nobody had seen the script, and I didn't think Harry Stratton would be happy to be wiped out in the first reel.

Jake, Dan and Timothy arrived at the pub just before opening time. They took their drinks into the snug and left me to deal with the early crowd. Just as well I knew all their orders off by heart.

Louie phoned at eight wanting to know what had happened. I fetched Dan but didn't learn much from his half of the conversation. I didn't like being excluded either. I'd done my bit, answered the summons and all that. Dan came to help out at nine and told me to make some sandwiches for Jake and Timothy. I told him they could make their own damn sandwiches, as I was going for a walk. The look on Dan's face hurt me but I went out anyway.

The night was clear. Stars stood out against the darkness blinking and flickering. I wished I was acting in a film; at least then I'd be able to walk away at the end of the night. I could sense that I'd reached some sort of turning-point. Decisions would be required of me shortly which would affect the rest of my life. I leant on the corner by the bus station smoking a Woodbine and just looking at the pub from the outside. When the hand fell on my shoulder I nearly wet myself.

Colm smiled down at me, looking like someone from another time, another place. I took his hand and walked across the road to the pub with him. Did I see him as a knight in shining armour or just someone I could hold on to? I can't say, as I gave it little thought, just did what came naturally. He had come back to see me, he wanted me; that was enough at that moment.

I want you as well, God said. Will you take My hand?

Your price is too high, I replied.

Wait till you see *his* shopping list, God snorted.

TWENTY-TWO

COLM DROPPED HIS suitcase behind the bar and immediately took charge while I ushered Dan into the snug. That was one of the great things about Colm, I didn't need to spell things out for him. Jake and Timothy sat like statues made from jelly. Very still but quivering now and then. When I entered the room behind Dan they looked indignant.

"She won't let go," Dan said as if he were talking about a problem child.

"Bernadette," Jake said, "we're in the shit and we're trying our damnedest to keep you out of it. Will you just go and serve bar and put this lot out of your mind."

"No," I said. "I'm in it, whatever it is, as much as all of you. And if I'm going to be implicated anyway, then I want the chance to have my say. So tell me."

They sighed wearily and exchanged glances which said "fuck it". I could see they were all tired and wanting to dig holes for themselves to hide in. I knew the feeling.

"Well?" I prompted.

"Philip has agreed the deal with Stratton. He gets paid tomorrow and then that's it. He was just telling the girls when I walked in. They couldn't believe what they were hearing at first, but when they finally took it in they flew at him and Janice. I got them reasonably calmed down and Philip and Janice into seats, then Nancy arrived downstairs, disturbed by all the noise. She wouldn't go back upstairs so we had to talk in a sort of code. Anyway, what it all boiled down to was the fact that the girls had two days to clear out of the house and into one of Stratton's places. He'd told Philip to tell the girls to expect a visit from him the next day, that's tomorrow, when he would fill them in on his way of operating. He also made it clear that Deirdre and Louie would be put in separate establishments to work, as he didn't like alliances forming between the girls." Dan took a swig of beer, shaking his head slowly as if to wipe out an image he didn't like. "I'll tell you, Bernie, I felt as if I was present at a slave auction. Philip was talking about the girls like they were just slabs of meat and Janice was worse. She just kept chipping in and saying that they should be grateful they weren't being turned out on to the streets, where they belonged. She wouldn't tone her language down even though Nancy was sitting there. I tried making a deal with Philip, said I'd pay him whatever Stratton had offered to get the girls off the hook. It was like talking to that wall. He couldn't even consider it; said Stratton would have his balls for dog meat if he did that." Dan sat back in his chair and wiped the sweat off his forehead. "I think I just flipped then. Nancy had gone off to the toilet and I just grabbed Philip and told Louie to hold on to Janice. Deirdre caught on straight away and hunted round for things to tie them up with. But even then Philip wouldn't budge. He kept saying that if we let him go and just left things the way they were, he wouldn't say anything to Stratton about my interference. I knew he was lying and looking at Janice I was certain that she'd be on the phone to Stratton the minute they were released."

There was a long pause when Dan finished his tale. I believed every word he said, no matter how appalling it sounded. No matter how much it seemed to come from another era. It looked as if the girls had no choice in the matter any longer. I'd never seen Stratton but the very thought of him sent goose-pimples as big as orange pips all over my body.

"So?" I said at last.

"So," said Jake after a furtive glance at the other two. "So the bastards are still tied up at the house and we're trying to work out what to do. If we let them go, the girls will be in immediate danger. Philip knows where the pub is, and he knows where Billy's flat is. Stratton won't just be satisfied to get the girls back; he'll have to do some sort of attack on Dan at least. Retribution. He couldn't let it get out that a few Paddies had bested him."

Timothy O'Keefe said nothing. He was definitely out of his depth. A few bets on the horses were the extent of his involvement with risk. This was altogether beyond his resources, but I could see he wasn't going to run away from it. He would stand by any decision that was made. I had an awful feeling that I would be the one who would want to run, who perhaps should run. Our choices were limited. It was a toss-up between Philip and Janice and Deirdre, Louie and Nancy. No one in the room was in any doubt where their allegiance lay. But time was short. Stratton was due at their house the following day. If we were to do anything useful, it had to be done swiftly.

I left the three of them in the snug glowering over their beer and joined Colm for the last rush. In between serving, collecting glasses and making small talk with the customers, I filled Colm in on the situation. Maybe a new mind on it would see a different perspective, a way out. It was a slim hope, but he listened with patience to all the ins and outs with a strange expression on his face.

At midnight Colm, myself and the three others sat drinking strong coffee in the bar. Decision time. Colm expressed clearly and succinctly what we already knew.

"We'll have to get rid of them," he said. Everyone nodded agreement between gulps for air. We were talking about murder. We were talking about the prospect of twenty years or more in prison if we were caught. There was no alternative. I remember the only relief I felt in the situation came from knowing that Philip and Janice were childless.

"We'll have to burn the house down with them in it," Jake said. I sensed he saw himself in competition with Colm, who was remarkably calm in the face of everyone else's agitation. "I'll do the job," Jake finished.

"No," Colm said. "You're known round there; you're associated with Philip. It has to be someone who can't be easily connected, and out of this gathering that means me."

I think it was the detached way in which Colm said it that set me off. All the old Catholic guilt and fear started grabbing at my insides, squeezing and pulling until I thought I would collapse. By the time I felt the beads of sweat on my upper lip it was too late. I tried to stand, but my legs weren't having any of it. Instead of making a dignified exit I fell forwards on to the table, knocking everything flying. Someone started to lift me up very gently. It was then that I started vomiting. The retching was so violent that I thought my insides would be wrecked for ever. To cap it all, I fainted into a pile of my own recycled dinner.

I came to some time afterwards. I was in my own bed with a hot-water bottle and Dan was stroking my forehead with a cool flannel.

"You'll be all right in a minute," Dan said. "Just lie still now."

I could see Timothy standing in the shadows of the room, but Jake and Colm were nowhere in sight.

"What's happening . . . where's Colm and . . ." I began, but Dan interrupted.

"Be still, will you," he said quietly. "The less you know, the better it is."

"But . . ."

"Never mind 'but'. Sure we all know you would have played your part, but it's best this way. Believe me."

My head sank back into the pillow as the side doorbell began ringing. Dan signalled for Timothy to keep an eye on me. When he came over into the light, he looked as green around the gills as I felt. Dan was back in an instant.

"It's Molloy," he said. "Best alibi we could get." He indicated for Timothy to go down. "Get the cards out, Tim, and start dealing." Then he turned to me. "Jake and Colm will be back shortly and they'll slip up here to see you when they see the lights on in the snug. Tell Jake to make like he's just up out of your bed and get him to amble down and show his face. Colm, well, I don't know, perhaps he should just stay hidden for now."

I nodded slowly, fearful that my stomach would erupt again if I moved too quickly. As Dan's feet receded down the stairs I felt a fresh attack of panic. I should have stopped them. There must have been another solution. Oh God, are you listening to me now? Will you stop them? Will you find a way to stop Stratton? Without realising it I'd put my hands together, prayer-fashion. Well, it was an emergency. Ever so slowly I slipped out of bed and on to my knees. Is this where you want me, God, eh? Well, here I am. Please, please, make a divine intervention. Please put an end to this craziness.

Jake's hands on my shoulders brought me back to reality. One glance at his face told me the deed had been done. Jake would bear the scar for the rest of his life. Sod You, God!

I told Jake what Dan had suggested, and he told me that Colm had gone off into the night and said not to worry.

Not to worry . . . Jesus, Mary and Joseph!

Colm's suitcase was still behind the bar next morning but there was no sign of him. The card game had gone on till four, so I was the only one up at seven. Molloy had stumbled home. The postman knocking startled me so much that I broke five pint glasses when I jumped. A parcel for Dan from Yorkshire. More books from his pal, I guessed, and a letter for me from Breda. It said:

> Mick and I had a baby girl on Thursday last. Eight pounds three ounces and perfectly beautiful. She is called Bridget Isobel, after my gran and yours. Mick never got on with his! Hope you can visit soon,
> Love Breda

Through the women it passes on. "Good luck, Breda," I said out loud.

"And good luck to yourself," Colm said from behind me.

The details don't matter. Neighbours in the street at Selly Oak were horrified at the suggestion in one newspaper that the house had been used as a brothel. Impossible, they said. They would have known.

Foul play was not suspected. The owner of the house and his wife were asleep in bed. It seems there were signs that they had been drinking heavily before falling asleep, which explained why they didn't wake up and attempt to escape the blaze.

We didn't congratulate ourselves. We did, however, breathe more easily. It was decided that I would accompany Noleen home and take the opportunity to see Breda and the baby. I think the lads thought I needed a break, except Colm that is. His plan, not previously discussed with me I might add, was for me to move south with him and set up home. He had a job with a large brick company and was offering me the role of kept woman.

I went to Ireland with Noleen. I needed to escape my guilt by doing something worthwhile. Visiting Breda, Mum and Dad and depositing Noleen home safely would help. As for God, He'd cooked his goose with me good and proper.

He said, Satan has tricks up his sleeve; he has honey to offer in the short term. Goodness is a difficult commodity to sell and it's getting worse, He said. I told Him He needed a better marketing department and He offered me the job. No thanks.

TWENTY-THREE

EVERYONE, INCLUDING COLM, Louie and Deirdre, chipped in for my fare and some spending money. I bought an old teddy bear with a magnetic grin from a secondhand shop in Sparkbrook for Breda's baby. I reckoned she would grow to love it with a passion. Deirdre sent more letters home; God only knows what tales she was telling. Deirdre's main worry when I visited her before leaving was that Noleen would spill the beans about her pregnancy. I was entrusted with the thankless task of trying to persuade Noleen to keep her mouth shut. Personally, I thought Jesus himself would have difficulty with that task. Water to wine, okay; Noleen and gossip, no way. My only hope was that she would be too stunned to remember anything clearly. Faint hope, indeed.

Colm made me promise to consider his proposition seriously while I was away. I felt bad having roped him in to the conspiracy against Philip and Janice, but he was a big lad and I hadn't held a gun to his head. He said I should take a chance with him, make a break from the desperation of the city and its awful memories. There was sense in what he said. I'd just never thought of myself as a sensible person on the whole.

I'd seen and heard enough of family life to put me off for good. It seemed to me that it was a question of control: someone always wanted to be in charge. Well, that's all very well if they're some sort of god, infallible, all-seeing, but I'd seen the appalling things that could be done in the name of various gods and I wasn't impressed. And yet sometimes of an evening I'd strolled round the streets in Selly Oak, Sparkbrook, Sparkhill, and glanced into other people's lives and felt a loneliness sweep over me. To be part of, to belong, was a strong urge, fight it though I did. Fear of rejection? Doubts about the fulfilling of expectations? Yes.

It wasn't such great fun feeling odd, feeling out of step with those around and beyond me, and I'd felt it since I was very young. Would it end in tears, as Grandma May often used to say when she accused me of being headstrong and impudent?

Timothy O'Keefe decided to go south with Colm, in the hopes of a job with the same company and to escape from memories of that night which seemed to hound him constantly. He was a delicate soul beneath all his bluff. I wished him well. Jake, severely annoyed about my relationship with Colm, moved in with Deirdre and Louie and visited Rita on her days off. I heard as I was leaving that she'd got him a job as a hospital porter. Strange happenings. Still, he would be a good tonic for all those patients going to face the surgeon's scalpel. The lad had charm and he had appeal. He just found loyalty and fidelity difficult to come by.

Noleen barely said a word all the way to Liverpool. I took the opportunity to review where I was at and where I might possibly be going. I felt grief at the loss of Tom. The things we would never now say to one another; the experiences we wouldn't share; the places we'd never visit.

I could find no real pity for Billy, so connected as he was in the loss of Tom. I knew I would never visit him again. He was lost to me as surely as Tom was. Something in me still wanted to know what Hawkins had done to get Billy's allegiance, but Molloy was on to that and he was far better equipped.

As the boat pulled out of the dock Noleen began to come to life again, with a vengeance! She bought half a bottle of gin and pinned me in a corner of the lounge. It seemed the closer she got to home, the stronger she felt.

"Why wasn't I informed that Deirdre was having Billy's baby?" she began. Talk about direct action. I was unprepared for this frontal assault. "I'll tell you why," she continued, "because it's not his child, is it? He wrote me months ago that Deirdre had stopped sleeping with him, and asking for advice on the matter. So. That wild man, Maloney, pretending to be a pal and then sneaking to Deirdre's bed behind Billy's back. Once a tinker, always a tinker." A flash of enlightenment from an unlikely source?

"And just what makes you think Jake is responsible, Noleen?" I demanded.

"Sure, Billy told me himself. There was a letter written to me but not posted in the pocket of his best jacket. I found it when me and Rita went to collect some things for him. Billy was evil about it. I'm surprised it was Deirdre he went for that night. I'd have thought Maloney would have been the target from the sounds of his letter."

Illumination indeed. Was that what Hawkins had fed to Billy?

"Did Billy say why he thought Jake was the culprit?" I asked.

"He said he was told by certain people in a position to know these things. That's good enough for me." She was halfway through the gin bottle and building up a fine head of steam. "Won't your mam be surprised to know the story," she went on, glancing at me out of the corner of a gin-bright eye. I looked at her carefully then, for the first time that day. She was wearing a hand-knitted twin set the colour of a muddy stream, a tweed skirt in a mixture of blue and green, black court shoes and thick tan stockings. At her neck hung a gold crucifix. I knew that I was playing for time and I think she did too. But though she had the cunning of a weasel, I knew she still had the mind of a superstitious peasant.

"That crucifix should burn a hole in your jumper for talking like that, Noleen. I'm surprised that a staunch woman of the Church could harbour such mean and devious thoughts," I said. I was making it up as I went along. "Does God smile kindly on those who willingly inflict pain and suffering on others? Does He turn a blind eye to persons who speak His name in reverent whispers and then behind His back stick the knife into other members of his flock?" I could tell by her face that I was hitting home. I continued to strike while the iron was glowing. "You know and I know, Noleen, that Mam is one of God's keenest supporters, and not just on high days and holidays. I'm bewildered that you're willing to lose such favour with Him up there for the sake of a bit of gossip." I got up immediately after I'd finished my speech and went to the toilet, leaving Noleen space to digest the sermon. I'd have made a damn good priest, even though I say it myself. But would it work? That was the question.

Back in the lounge Noleen was not alone. There was a small, dapper fellow with light, curly hair sitting with her. He put me in mind of the actor, James Cagney. I watched them from a distance. They made an odd couple: Noleen with her comfortable clothes and he with his spiv's uniform. The kipper tie even had a naked lady on it. As Noleen saw me approaching she pulled her hand free from his and smoothed down the tweed skirt which had risen above her knees. I recognised the flush on her cheeks. It could have been the drink, but it wasn't; it was sexual arousal. It matched the expression on his face. I admit to being shocked. Shocked and amused at the same time.

"Bernadette," she said in a dainty voice. "This is Kevin Lynch, an old friend of mine from Dungarvan."

Kevin Lynch was clearly annoyed at the interruption to his advances to Noleen but he pulled himself together well enough.

"Pleased to meet to you, Bernadette," he said. "Are you home for long?"

"That's yet to be decided. A lot depends on the condition of my mother," I said, with a pointed look at Noleen.

"Is she unwell?" he asked.

"There's rumours that she might be getting some bad news."

"Ah well," he said sagely. "Won't you have a little drink with us?"

I accepted a drop of whisky and settled back to observe the mating ritual.

"Noleen was just telling me about how well her son is doing over in England in the business field," he said.

Noleen nearly choked on her drink. Kevin patted her

back, and as he did the chain holding her crucifix came loose and the whole thing dropped into Noleen's glass of gin. She dropped the glass with a gasp and ran across the lounge to the steps leading up to the deck. Kevin mumbled something about sea legs and swiftly followed her. Just as well, because I fell into a fit of laughter which lasted a good two minutes.

I retrieved the crucifix and chain from the floor and wiped it clean. Did God have a sense of humour after all? Half an hour later neither Noleen nor Kevin had returned. I gathered our various belongings into a heap, put a cushion over them and tried to sleep. I couldn't. All I could think of was that I'd helped to murder two people and here I was barely a week later not giving the event more than a second's thought. Noleen's crucifix felt hot in my sweaty palm. I put it safely in my pocket. Out of sight, out of mind. I see everything, God said. I told Him to go and bother someone else.

I asked a friendly looking woman with two children fast asleep on her lap to keep an eye on our stuff and followed Noleen and Kevin up on deck. By rights they ought to be frozen to the bone. The sea was rough but not splashing the decks as it had been on my last trip. There were no stars to be seen. One or two people were up and about, but not a sign of my missing companions at first. When I did find them I wished I hadn't. They were under an oily tarpaulin going at it like tigers.

I felt the same as I would have had I ever come across Father Molloy and Molly Cahill in the same mode. Like God had deserted me good and proper. I left the scene of the activity without a word. Mainly because I couldn't think of a suitable word apart from "fuck", and that seemed an understatement in the circumstances. Anyway, I thought as I curled up in the lounge once more, Noleen would be easier to handle with that knowledge under my belt.

Irish-Catholic hypocrisy seemed to have a sharper sting than any other, maybe because there was a part of me that wished it wasn't so, that wanted so much to be able to believe. Sexual matters had always been taboo at home, nevertheless me and Breda knew about how frequently girls in service were molested and raped; we knew about priests being "at it"; we knew about fathers and brothers who used their own children for sexual pleasure. We also knew that these very same people took communion on Sundays without flinching. The church roof never fell in on them. So Noleen's two-facedness was no surprise. In a way I wished her well of it.

I woke up around six to the distant sound of Dublin. Noleen and Kevin were already awake, washed and groomed, and sitting like children, opposite one another with their knees touching. My return to consciousness was an unwelcome distraction by the looks on their faces. I padded off to the toilets without more than a nod in their direction. My mouth tasted like last week's dog's dinner. Noleen followed me. She certainly knew how to get people at awkward moments.

"I've decided," she said softly, "to put the whole experience of England behind me. I don't want to remember anything about the place. I shall visit Billy from time to time, of course, and write to him regularly."

"Asking him about his business interests, of course," I

said through my toothbrush. I bit my tongue. It hurt. God is always watching! Noleen continued her speech as if she hadn't heard me.

"Kevin and I are going to be married as soon as possible. He has come home to open a small restaurant in Cappoquin. We shall run it together as a joint venture." If I was any judge, I knew who would be putting up most of the money, and it wasn't Kevin. Still, maybe she needed someone else to mother now that she'd decided to abandon Billy to the heathen sharks. "As far as the family at home are concerned, I shall be grateful if you will support my story as to Billy's condition and activities," she went on. "In return I shall keep my mouth shut about Deirdre and everything else I suspect is going on in that place over there."

She didn't wait for a reply, just marched out with her bag over her arm. I called her back as she reached the door and held out her chain and crucifix.

"Give it to Breda for the baby," Noleen said before she turned heel and disappeared. I certainly wouldn't give it to Breda for the baby, I thought to myself. The poor child will be surrounded by enough icons without that hanging around her neck. As I turned back to the washbasin I banged my knee. The pain shot up my leg as if I'd been scalded. God works in mysterious ways all right! Or was Satan in control just now? Cause and effect, God said. I could tell He was laughing.

— TWENTY-FOUR —

THE LAST I saw of Noleen and Kevin was their backs hurrying down the gangplank, several dozen people in front of me, into a misty Dublin morning. Fine chaperone I turned out to be! Still, it was a huge relief to have got all that potential mayhem sorted so easily, even if, as a piece of fiction, no one would ever believe it.

Well then, there was a solution as to how Hawkins had managed too wind Billy up to breaking point. I had assumed that Billy knew the true story of Deirdre's pregnancy, but perhaps he preferred Hawkins' version of events. I made a mental note to ask Deirdre about it at some later date.

I felt myself moving closer to Isobel's sphere of influence with every mile the train covered. It was a comforting feeling. Continuity of sorts; magic and mystery definitely; unspoken words almost certainly.

It was late afternoon when I got in sight of home. My lift from Clonmel had dropped me at Flynn's corner, so I walked the last few miles slowly, gathering the sense of the place about myself. I felt good, glad to be walking the same steps I'd walked often in the past. Pleased to see the landmarks which were irreversibly written on my brain. But glad also that I'd left. Even Rafferty's bull, old now and certainly senile, made me smile as he went through the motions of stamping and snorting. Once he had been

the terror of my childhood dreams, cloven-hoofed and
horned as he was.

I rounded the last bend before the house. Up to my left
the long drive which led to Andersons' house, almost the
very spot where Grandad Joseph had been wounded. I
paced in his footsteps as I neared the house; could almost
feel my legs staggering as I reached for the latch; nearly
see the pool of blood he made on the kitchen floor; hear
the next round of shots which finished him off; see Isobel
running up towards the murderers, risking her own life to
stop any more bullets hitting her man.

It wasn't nostalgia or sentimentality I was experiencing.
It was more a placing of myself in some sort of chronology,
of understanding that there was continuity of a kind even
though I might so frequently feel displaced.

Dad was seated in his usual spot. He looked up at me
when I entered, gave a slight nod and turned back to his
paper. What else had I expected? Mam came out of the
back kitchen, her hands thick with flour.

"Bernadette," she said. I strained to hear a catch in her
throat, any sign, however small, that emotion lurked there
somewhere. And I think I did. So sure of it was I that I
dropped my bag and rushed towards her. I put my head
on her breast and listened to her heart pumping as I must
have done when I was in the womb. I wanted to rock her
in my arms and tell her I didn't blame her, that it wasn't
her fault she couldn't love me.

She let my head rest there for a few moments, but her
hands hovered in the air behind my back. It could have
been because she didn't want to put flour on me. It could
have been.

"Any message from Deirdre?" Dad said into the silence. Back to normality.

I glanced quickly at Mam and Dad, wondering if I dare tell them that it was all right; that I forgave them for their coldness to me; that I was sorry for all the pain that Mam had endured; that Dad had done right to love her so much. But we were a family unused to discussion, unfamiliar with intimacy. I doubted if anything I was to say could alter that. In fact it might only add to the problem.

I fished in my bag for Deirdre's letter. As I handed it to him I stared at the top of his head, hoping maybe to bore my way into his consciousness from a new angle.

"Did you get my letter?" I asked.

"I did," he answered. He rose then, as if to escape further questions, took the paraffin lamp off its hook and went out into the yard. I knew he was going into the peat shed to read Deirdre's letter in peace and quiet, just as Mam went into the bedroom when I gave her her letter. Left alone in the kitchen I wanted to shout at the top of my voice: "DEIRDRE IS A WHORE! I AM A MURDERER!" I couldn't, of course. I knew for certain that the wrath of God would come tumbling down in the shape of Dad's strap. He would have no trouble believing me a murderer, but Deirdre a whore? Never.

But they had to take some blame, didn't they? Surely it was their example which had set me and Deirdre in opposition right from the start. Had made us different but not equal. In loving her so much they'd set high expectations for her. Perhaps too high.

Next morning fresh soda bread, milk and butter were set out on the table but the kitchen was empty. Was this the way it was to be? A picture I used to love of a circle of sweet-faced cherubs looked down on me as I ate. I wanted to turn it to the wall, so obscenely innocent and content the faces seemed to be. I went to the stream in the garden to wash. The water was sharp and icy, just what I needed to start the day off well. Mam didn't like me washing in the stream. Always said it was unseemly. I was being a petulant child again, seeking a reaction. Any kind of reaction rather than the meanness of silence. No one came. Only the goat paid me any attention, peeping at me from round the back of the shed. I gazed at the house. It was so small to have borne so many children, seen so many sorrows, but it must have had the joys as well or else it would have crumbled to dust in agony.

I dressed carefully. I wanted so much to make a good impression on Bridget Isobel Kelly, my best friend's baby. I dug out the teddy bear. Cute. Thought twice about Noleen's crucifix but still rejected it and set out with a brisk stride. Father Molloy nearly knocked me in the ditch with his old car. He'd always been a notoriously bad driver, even with a horse and cart. He pulled to a sudden halt about fifty yards ahead of me, opened the driver's door and started to reverse back towards me. I was in fear for my life and not without cause. If I hadn't moved hurriedly out of the way, he would have driven over my feet at the very least.

"Bernadette Murphy," he said. "Back again so soon. You'll be coming to confession tomorrow I take it." He'd always had a thing about confession. Unkind souls had often suggested he got his kicks out of listening to the catalogue of impure thoughts and deeds. A confession from me would probably roast his eardrums.

"Not tomorrow, Father," I said, "but sometime I'd like to have a talk with you."

His eyes were bright and intelligent as he looked me over. I doubted there were many flies on him. He liked to give the impression of slight madness, minor eccentricity, but he was the full shilling, of that I had no doubt. But could I dare to breach such very mortal subjects as birth and death with him?

"Bernadette," he said, "I really think that anything you need to talk to me about should be said in the confessional. That way I'm sworn to secrecy. Wouldn't that be a better solution all round?"

Sharp as sugar, sure enough. He drove off in an explosion of dust. Never entered his head to give me a lift. Nothing personal. He never picked anyone up unless they were ill or injured. We all have our little imperfections. Perhaps I would be forced to the confessional in the end. Bless me, Father, for I have sinned . . .

Breda had the baby on the breast when I arrived. Madonna and child. She'd let her chestnut hair grow longer. It rolled over her shoulders and nestled in the baby's neck. She looked entirely happy.

"Is it what you thought it would be like?" I asked.

"And more," she said. "No one told me just how much I would love her."

"I don't suppose anyone can explain that," I said.

Mick came in and made tea for us while I watched Breda and answered her questions about Deirdre with lies. No point in expecting Breda to share that particular burden. I felt bad though. It was the first time I'd ever lied to her. Breda was really just the same as ever, more lovely if anything, but I couldn't help feeling excluded. There was her and the baby and Mick, and then there was me. Outsider. Interloper. Misfit.

Come back to Me, God said. I will welcome you into the bosom of My Church. You shall have laws to obey, duties to perform; everything will be clearly mapped out.

Yes, I replied, as long as I'm prepared to be a second-class citizen. Isn't that it? Second only to God and submissive to man, He responded. Exactly, I said.

TWENTY-FIVE

THE DAYS SEEMED to have too many hours. Up early and late to bed. Mam and Dad were adept at avoiding me and meals we had together were mostly silent. I walked a lot, sat in the hen house, visited Breda and felt very isolated.

Colm wrote a letter declaring desperate love for me. I wondered how many of those he'd written to other women. Unfair? Not at all. Most men are looking for a new mammy to replace the one they've left. Especially Irish men. Though why Colm should see me as mother material I had no idea. He'd got Timothy fixed up at the brick company and they were sharing a flat. But, Colm assured me, he was on the lookout for a nice little house to share with me. I admit there was something attractive about the idea of a nice little house to play in. Where I could scrub and polish and wash and iron and cook and fall into Colm's arms at a minute's notice, but something inside kept telling me it would never work. He would grow bored and I would be left behind. He was too beautiful not to be tempted by grass that looked greener and by God I certainly was no Venus de Milo. It didn't enter my head that I was the one who might get bored. I thought I'd be too busy working at the million tasks a house requires. Then at the end of his letter he hinted at the idea of a large family for us. No, I certainly wasn't

ready for that. Then I'd be left with children to rear alone
and no prospect of escape for years to come.

I wrote a brief reply saying I hoped he was well and
answering none of the questions he'd asked.

A week into my stay I went to the church for the first
time, not to mass or confession or anything, just to be in
the cool and quiet of it. For a long time I sat on a bench
drawing in the smell of the incense, staring at the windows
and the statues, trying to remember how I'd felt about
them long before when I'd believed in the wisdom of
God. I couldn't recapture it, but when I got down on my
knees and closed my eyes I felt at peace. I was disturbed
by a woman of about sixty shuffling up the aisle. She went
to light a candle, then shuffled to sit at a bench nearby. She
was a stranger to me and dressed as if she was a visitor.
We got up to leave at more or less the same time and I
waited to walk out with her. No harm in being friendly.

There was an old black car waiting for her outside; an
impatient young man sat at the wheel.

"My grandson, Dermot," the woman said. "I used to
work round these parts when I was younger, and he's
giving me a tour. I'm enjoying it, but I don't think he is.
Still, I loaned him the money for the car so I have some say."

She asked me about my family, as is the custom, and
her face lit up with delight as I reeled them off.

"So Kathleen Murphy is your mother?" she said. I
nodded. "What a coincidence. I worked in the same house
as her in Thomastown at one time. I was cook and she
was a maid. What a fine-looking girl she was, wild as
mountain strawberries, with a tongue like a lash. All the
lads were mad for her."

Dermot tooted the horn of the car impatiently.

"Tell Kathleen I was asking after her, won't you?" she said, before she hobbled to the car.

I'd never heard my mother described as wild before. I'd never witnessed her as anything but organised and dependable. In fact I'd never even wondered what she might have been like at my age. She was Mam and that was it. Perhaps she'd had to compromise much more than I'd ever realised. Perhaps her and me and Deirdre were similar after all.

As I walked up the hill to O'Malley's shop to buy stamps the sky opened up. I was soaked to the skin within minutes. Mrs O'Malley took me in the back parlour to the fire and handed me clean towels. She put the kettle on, sliced home-baked ginger cake and insisted I tell her all about England. Was it true people didn't speak to one another in the streets? Was it true there was very little green land to speak of? That the buses sometimes had two levels, like a house? When I left the comfort of Mrs O'Malley's parlour I was almost dry, apart from soggy shoes. I walked home breathing in the fresh smells created by the rain, watching drops of water hovering and falling off branches on the tall trees that lined Kilsha. I recalled the times I'd sped down it on my bike, rushing to mass or to some rendezvous or other, not a real care in the world apart from the spoilt Deirdre. I thought of Mam's pregnancy and the agonies of conscience she must have gone through and I made the connection to Deirdre's state. Parallels, and me standing outside of it all trying to create some meaning, some sense, some explanation of where I fit in relation to it.

Grandma May always called me a dreamer, as if it was the worst thing in the world to be. She said it out of the corner of her mouth like she couldn't bear to give it too much space. Once when she was angry with me she bit her clay pipe in two, and I laughed myself hoarse until she got hold of me by the hair and thrashed me with her coarse, calloused hands.

Is that what we miss when we're away from home, that simplicity that was to do with childhood and not just the place we lived? That time when it seemed everything was ahead of you and if you were lucky you hadn't come face to face with real evil or even true disappointment?

As I opened the latch on the kitchen door I caught the sound of sobbing. I rushed in. There was Noleen wringing her hands and weeping a waterfall. She was sitting in Dad's chair as he stood awkwardly by the table. Mam was comforting Noleen and offering her tea. Noleen shot me such a look of hatred as I walked in that I was sure that the cat was out of the bag good and proper. She'd spilled the beans and I was in for a pile of pain. I even thought of walking straight back out again and seeking refuge at Breda's. I wondered if flyboy Kevin had gone off with her money and she was here seeking compensation out of my hide.

Noleen got control of herself eventually. I just sat at the end of the table waiting for hell to arrive. Eventually Mam broke the silence.

"Noleen's had some bad news," she said. "Your cousin Billy has been killed in a car accident."

Noleen watched to see how I was reacting. I wasn't. Something told me I was hearing a filtered version of the truth. It didn't matter, Billy was probably better off dead. At least he'd have peace.

"I'm sorry to hear it, Noleen," I said. It was expected of me.

The wailing and comforting went on for some time. Dad went off and bought some gin and things got mellower. Time to think of the past, the way Billy used to be. "Remember the time he followed me when I was feeding that bad-tempered sow who'd just had a litter and she nearly bit his leg off? Remember how his hair used to curl on to his forehead and it would not stay back even if you nailed it down? Remember how he used to run and hide whenever Timmon came back on his cart; he thought he looked like the devil?" I listened patiently. I didn't mind reminiscing.

Some time later I noticed Dad making the usual preliminary movements he made before going to bed. Folding the paper neatly and putting it on the window ledge. Poking the fire thoroughly. Checking the amount of tobacco in his pouch before putting it in the dresser drawer.

"D'you remember what I was like as a child, Noleen?" I chirped up.

"Like a changeling. Something the fairies might have delivered for a bit of mischief," she replied, with a drunken wink at Mam. Mam gave me that warning look I knew so well, and before I could open my mouth Noleen was off on a tale about how Uncle Liam had dug up a fairy ring and infected his hand so badly he nearly lost it and had to make recompense to the little people before it would get better.

Dad slipped off to bed midway through the recollection. Mam swiftly followed, leaving me and Noleen staring into the fire, contemplating our own personal memories of Billy.

TWENTY-SIX

I DON'T THINK anyone slept terribly well that night. Too much history drifting in and out of the rooms, whistling up the chimney, creeping between the chinks in the house's armour. I dreamed about Isobel and let her know that I suspected God's opinion of women. She replied that the Holy Ghost was without a doubt a woman like myself and so I should direct my prayers to that quarter. It got me thinking about the Virgin Mary. Had she wanted God to visit her with His sacred sperm? Had she wanted to carry this child of a stranger for nine months? Had she any choice at all in the matter? A peasant woman faced with an authoritative and powerful male who wanted His way with her. What had Joseph thought of the baby Jesus? Had he seen Him as an interloper? Did it matter? Baby Jesus soon became a man and as a man had no doubt about His own worth, even though He'd been conceived in the strangest of circumstances. So, if I'd been born a boy, would things have turned out differently?

Noleen dragged me out of my contemplation to tell me Kevin had arrived to take her back to Cappoquin and handed me a letter while putting her fingers to her lips. Secrets. I strolled into the kitchen after pulling my old dressing-gown over my shoulders. I was surprised at the change in Kevin. Gone was the spiv and in his place the very epitome of a gentleman farmer. He looked like he was having a great time.

They invited me over to stay with them any time I liked before I went back to England. It was a sincere invitation I think, me being the only one in Ireland who knew the truth about Billy.

I looked at the severe faces of Mam and Dad and suddenly wanted to get out of the house. "Would you wait a couple of minutes?" I asked Noleen. "I've remembered I have an appointment with Father Molloy. You could drop me down there, couldn't you?"

There was a bit of tut-tutting and standing about, but five minutes later I was being driven at breakneck speed down Kilsha towards God's representative. Father Molloy was just walking across to the church to take confession when we arrived.

"There you are, Bernadette," he said matter of factly. "Hurry along now and you'll be the first of the day."

I was alone in the church, but the pews soon filled up. Breda came and sat beside me. I wondered what the hell she could possibly have to confess to anybody. When Father Molloy signalled that he was ready I couldn't budge. It wasn't fear of the Lord which overcame me; it was the thought of all the other confessors having to sit while I poured out my store of mortal sins. I waited until there was only Breda and myself left and when she went in I looked at the letter Noleen had given me. It was from Deirdre.

"Billy found dead. Hanged himself with knotted sheets."

That was it. No "Dear Noleen", no "Love Deirdre". There's no doubt the girl had a cool head. Cold, you might even suspect.

At last there was no more delay. Breda seemed to have been given a big penance. I wondered again what she could possibly have done. In the confessional box Father Molloy pulled back the curtain. I could see his profile through the screen as I had on so many occasions in the past.

"Bless me, Father, for I have sinned," I began. He interrupted me.

"Just get on with it, Bernadette," he said. "We haven't the whole day to waste." So much for the sanctity of the confessional. Was he still sworn to secrecy if we didn't observe the proper form? He assured me he was. And so I told him. I didn't mention Deirdre or any of the others by name, just gave him the bare details. My mouth was dry when I finished talking. I was tempted to drink the holy water but that was sacrilege too great even for me.

Father Molloy was silent for some time. I began to wonder if he'd fallen asleep. I tapped the wire grill.

"Don't be so impatient, Bernadette!" he snapped. "Anyone would think this was the first confession of murder I ever heard. Well it's not. Far from it. So. I don't hear any sign of remorse from you. Are you not sorry for what you did?"

"I don't think so, Father. You see, there didn't seem to be any other choice."

"Only God has the right to decide who shall live or die. Now, He may have agreed with your decision had He been on the spot, but as He wasn't we'll never know. Well, not until the Day of Judgement anyway."

"Father, I thought God was everywhere, all the time?"

"He gets tied up just like everyone else. Now. If you're not genuinely sorry and asking God for forgiveness, then

I can't give you absolution."

"I'm not asking for absolution, Father. I just want to know what you think," I said firmly.

"Think?" he said, a note of surprise in his voice. "I don't think. I just carry out the word of the Lord. Now get out of here and do the stations of the cross twice and maybe God will talk to you Himself."

I didn't do the stations of the cross, of course, so I'll never know whether God would have done a visitation. I walked down by the river instead and wondered which spot it was that Mam had picked when she thought of drowning me and her all those years before. I was curiously relieved to have told Father Molloy the grim facts. A great thing, the confessional. If only I'd been really sorry for what I'd done, I could have been free of it by now and in a state of grace. The river was full, swollen by the rain. It looked inviting.

Back at home they were waiting for me. My bags were packed and set by the door. Mam on one side of the fire, Dad on the other, like two marble statues. Dad's eyes were cold. Mam's held something but it was too small for me to latch on to.

"The prodigal daughter, is it?" I said. "Will you kill the fatted calf when I come back?"

"You won't be coming back," Dad said. "Not while I'm alive anyway. Take your stuff and go back to England where you belong. You've never brought anything but suffering to this house."

It was the longest speech I'd ever heard him make. It hurt. Mam held my coat for me to put on. No discussion. At the gate I looked up and down the road. Breda's?

Cappoquin? The first car that came in sight was headed in the opposite direction, towards Cork. I flagged it down. Mam appeared beside me suddenly. She pressed a few pounds into my hand and squeezed it hard. Her eyes were full of tears. Small consolation.

A man with a plastic face tried to pick me up on the boat. He made me think of the Flynn brother that Isobel had told me about. Apparently the man used to piss in a pot at night time, then wash his face in it the following morning. For forty years. Isobel said that at the age of sixty his face was as smooth as a baby's bottom. Well, that's what this man's face was like.

I thought of Colm. The temptation to fall into his arms was stronger than ever. Another sort of oblivion. I wondered what it would be like to wake up next to him every morning, to snuggle against him every night. To make love as often and in as many different ways as we liked. That was allowed if you were man and wife. Come to think of it, he'd never mentioned marriage. In Liverpool I wrote a hurried note to Breda asking her to find out anything she could about Colm Connolly and send me the details as soon as possible. I'm sure Breda sometimes thought I was an egg short of a dozen, but I knew Mick went up near Athlone from time to time and could bend a few ears easily enough. No harm in asking.

Was I looking for some sort of conventional solution? Some sort of substitute daddy? Or did I just want to be needed, to escape from a reality that was just too raw to deal with.

I remembered how, at the missionary classes, Father Molloy used to say that there were no guarantees in life, that nothing was certain except that on the Day of Judgement God would call us all to task. No guarantees. No escape. And did I really have any desire to be responsible for anyone else — man or child, often both in the same body. Wasn't it difficult enough looking after myself, understanding my own complicated desires? I tried to concentrate on the Holy Ghost, wondered what She looked like, what She would think, how often She disagreed with God and Jesus. But still I felt this awful loneliness. Only Isobel had truly loved me and, if I couldn't learn to love myself, surely no one else ever would.

TWENTY-SEVEN

I CALLED AT Deirdre's before going to the pub. I was surprised at the size of her.

"When's it due?" I asked.

"Middle of next month." She grimaced.

Her and Louie and Jake had redecorated the flat and got a few new sticks of furniture. It looked much better, more homely, more lived in. Deirdre reluctantly made me a cup of tea. She didn't want me to stay, I could see that. I filled her in on the happenings at home, including Breda's baby. Stupid of me. She threw her cup at me as she screamed for me to shut up.

"You do it deliberately, you bitch!" she yelled at me.

"I don't," I said. "Really I don't. I just didn't think it through."

"Well get out and go and think it through somewhere else!"

At the door I stopped. Might as well get hung for a deer as a rabbit.

"Did Billy know how you got pregnant?" I asked.

"Of course he fucking did! Now piss off and don't come back in a hurry."

What a charmer. I didn't feel hurt by Deirdre any more, only numb and, I suppose, disappointed. As I walked down the path to the gate she called after me.

"Not satisfied with totally disrupting Mam and Dad,

you have to come back here and start meddling."

Enough is enough. "I recall that you didn't mind me meddling when you needed me."

"And I suppose you want love and gratitude for evermore, do you?"

I wanted love, yes, but I wasn't going to tell her that. Give her more weapons to attack me with? I think not. I couldn't hate her though; I knew she must be going through agony with every day that passed. The baby would have been making itself felt now for a while, kicking and stirring, stretching itself out ready for its assault on the world. It wasn't a situation I'd wish on anyone.

Back at the pub things had changed. I slipped in the rear and up to my room to unpack my things and have a wash before tackling the bar. It was no longer my room. Everything had been moved about. There were two beds instead of one, an extra chest of drawers and a new carpet. A set of child's drawings of matchbox houses, neat gardens and lollipop trees were pinned over one of the beds. Its quilt was covered in nursery rhymes. I didn't need to be told what had happened. Louie and Nancy had moved in.

If I'd felt bad being thrown out of home, I felt worse now. Part of me had always been rejected back there, but here I'd grown to believe I might really belong.

Never take anything for granted. Never. Louie appeared in the doorway as I stood on the spot, stunned and trying to get control.

"Like it?" she said. "Nancy does, much better then Billy's."

When I turned to face her she read my face accurately.

"Oh, Bernie, I'm sorry. I . . . we all thought you were moving in with Colm when you came back." She put her arms round me. "He's been telling everyone about the little house he's picked out for you and how great it's going to be. We just assumed . . ."

I pulled away from her and clattered into the bathroom. "Why didn't anyone ask me?" I shouted. "Have I no rights at all?"

I hid in the bathroom with my back against the door until I knew the bar would be empty. There was no way I could face that scene. Dan knocked on the door a few times before I felt strong enough to face him. All I could think was "Where do I go now?" And no answers would come.

Dan held his arms out to me when I entered the kitchen. I ignored the gesture and sat as far away from him as possible. Nancy was listening to the radio in her bedroom, "Journey into Space" or something. Louie was absent.

"Bernie," he said, "Colm was so convincing. I never for a minute doubted that you'd agreed. In fact I was hurt that you hadn't mentioned it to me." I said nothing.

My throat felt as if it had seized up. "And then things were getting difficult at Billy's. Nancy was beginning to ask awkward questions about the men callers, and what with Deirdre almost immovable and Louie and June trying to earn the money, well, there didn't seem any alternative . . ."

He tailed off, waiting for a response. "Christ all-fucking-mighty," I said. "Are they still on the game after all that's happened? You should have sense, even if they haven't. What about Stratton? They're operating right in the middle of his patch. Did we commit murder for nothing?"

"Ssh, ssh," Dan pleaded. He was looking towards Nancy's room. Nancy's room! "It was difficult for them, Bernie. Some of their old clients found out where they were and threatened to go to Stratton if they didn't set up shop again. And the bastard who made Deirdre pregnant . . ."

I interrupted him. "*Raped*!" I screamed. "He raped her!" Nancy came running then. Maybe that's what I had intended, to really upset him as he'd upset me. But all she said was, "Who's got all the grapes then?"

I paced around like a thing caged while Dan fussed over Nancy. Louie's away earning her honest bob or two, I thought spitefully. On one of my pacing rounds I noticed a letter addressed to me stuck behind the clock. The postmark was Yorkshire. It was from Joan:

> Dear Bernie,
>
> I got to thinking about you the other day after I'd seen a Maureen O'Hara film. It was a very weepy one and she reminded me of you somehow. I haven't heard from you in a while and I was wondering if you were coping all right down there.
>
> I've moved into a little house of my own now, it's got two spare bedrooms and a garden which I keep full of flowers. Do come and visit or at least drop a line to reassure me that you're keeping well. I hope you don't mind me worrying about you.
>
> My new address is overleaf, as is my phone number at the pit.
>
> Much love,
> Joan

So, maybe the Holy Ghost had been listening after all and maybe She looked a bit like Joan.

The letter cheered me up considerably. Somebody out there cared. I decided to spend a few nights in the snug so that I could warn Joan of my impending arrival. Fate taking charge again. I'd leave the whole lot of them behind in Birmingham. They had shut me out on the say-so of a comparative stranger. I trembled when I thought of what I would say to Colm Connolly when I saw him.

I worked in the pub that night. Why not? A few bob wouldn't go amiss. I was clearing glasses when Jake came in. He picked me up and swung me around the room, much to the delight of the customers, most of them too old to tackle a job like that themselves.

"Oh God," he said, "but it's great to see you. You've no idea how much I've missed you, and Louie says it's all nonsense about you moving away with Colm, Bernie, Bernie." He kept kissing me until my lips were sore and Dan ordered him to stop.

That was my trouble, you see, I thought to myself afterwards as I lay in the snug with Jake asleep beside me, I was starved of affection. And Jake was the great one for dishing that out. Wasn't he just.

Later, as morning began to highlight the dust on the snug tables and around the skirting boards, I began to feel less easygoing about the whole thing. Was I any better than Deirdre? Should I start charging for my services? I nudged Jake awake. He grumbled a great deal. So it is that romantic illusions are lost.

"Hey," I said. "It's never like this on the films the morning after."

He turned away from me, taking all the bedcovers
with him.

— TWENTY-EIGHT —

A WEEK LATER my back was aching from sleeping on the snug floor and no word from Joan. Feelings of rejection were creeping in again, together with envy at the easy and happy relationships I witnessed between Dan, Nancy and Louie. Desperation drove me to try and contact Joan by phone. It was with relief that I learned she was away on a week's holiday in Scarborough. I relaxed. She would contact me as soon as she returned I was sure.

Jake had cleared off back to Wolverhampton the day after our last brief encounter. I found I was sad that he'd gone but also relieved. One less problem to deal with.

Colm arrived at the pub on Friday evening. As he walked across the room towards me with a wide grin on his face, I kept reminding myself of the claim he'd made on me in my absence. He really was beautiful. If I wasn't very careful I'd end up making love to him without a sheath and then I'd really be in trouble. That would be his way. His method of attack.

He leaned over the bar, took both of my hands in his and just stared at me for several seconds. I don't know what the regulars made of all this attention I was getting. Perhaps it was better than the films for them. I stared back, all the while fighting the desire to have him wrap me in his ample arms and wipe away the cares of the world.

"I knew you'd be here when I came," he said breathlessly.

"I bought a ticket for you to come back down south with me on Sunday evening."

"Well you've wasted your money then," I replied. The cheek of the man!

"No, I don't think so, Bernie," he said with a grin. "You can't keep fighting it." I had to drag my hands out of his to serve a customer. I was glad of the bar between us, a barrier that I badly needed. He sat up at the corner of the counter with his bag on the floor beside him. There for the duration. He told me how Timothy had taken up with a really nice girl he'd met at a dance. They were going steady, he said, just like us! Where did the man get off being so sure of himself? I looked at Dan for some sort of support, but he was just grinning like an ass at the whole spectacle. Surely he hadn't read all those fairy tales about willing girls being swept off their feet and carried off on white horses. No, but he was a cinema addict and I knew he'd just been to see *The African Queen* with Humphrey Bogart and Katharine Hepburn for the second time. Romance enough for anyone. The worst part of it was that I wasn't at all sure I didn't want to be carried away, yet there was something holding me back.

Maybe it was thinking about Joan and the little talk she'd given me about love and lust. Maybe it was fear of my own desire. Maybe it was simply the fact that he was just too handsome for words and I felt like the ugly duckling next to him.

When Dan called time, Colm leaned over to me and said quietly, "We'll go up into the city tomorrow and I'll buy you a lovely dinner to celebrate and then we'll go hunting for a ring." A ring was it? But I had Isobel's ring, didn't I, and that was quite enough for me. Wasn't it?

As the customers drifted out, Molloy drifted in. It was some time since I'd seen him and I would hardly have recognised him if I'd bumped into him in the street. Gone was the round, smiling face, replaced by something gaunt and drawn. His clothes hung as if they were held together with bits of string. He must have lost a couple of stone in weight at least. Dan rushed from behind the bar to greet him and guide him to the table next to the fire. He nodded for me to bring brandy over.

I heard Molloy and Dan whispering as I cleared the tables and washed the glasses. Every so often Dan would exclaim "No" or "Jesus wept". Colm sat on, watching me, and every so often reaching out to touch me as I passed near him. What could he be after, pursuing me when he could have the pick of the bunch? I was weakening by the minute.

You always were weak, God said spitefully.

"Bernie," Molloy said, "come over here and sit down. I've things to talk to you about."

Colm followed me over. Molloy gave him a look which let me know that the Chief Inspector still lurked inside the altered frame.

"Alone," Molloy said to Colm. "I want Bernie on her own, pal. Make yourself scarce for a while."

Colm reacted very badly. He took hold of Molloy's collar and proceeded to pull him backwards out of the chair. It took Dan and Molloy together to get him out of the pub without someone getting hurt.

"That boy's on a short fuse, Bernie," Molloy said when he returned. "Is he yours?"

"He thinks he is," I said. "I'm not at all sure myself."

"He's just in love," Dan said indulgently. "You remember what that's like, don't you, Molloy?"

"Very vaguely," Molloy replied.

It was a long and complicated tale Molloy had to tell. The fiver I'd given him from Billy's envelope he'd traced back to a robbery the previous year. It seems that although Smith and Hawkins were not directly involved in any thefts they were getting a rake-off and, in order to keep up their record of arrests to cover this fact, they pulled in all sorts of characters who they knew would get no sympathy from magistrates and judges: travellers, tramps, bag ladies, blacks, Asians with hardly any knowledge of English. They got their arrest and conviction quota easily enough. The most disturbing aspect of it, which Molloy had uncovered, was that Smith and Hawkins both subscribed to a small right-wing, semi-military group run by an ex-major in the British army. Remnants of Mosley's British Union of Fascists, Molloy said, but covert in their operations because memories of Hitler were still at the forefront of people's minds. Molloy had gone to his superiors with his information, been given a verbal pat on the back and a week later charged with the very same offences he'd accused Smith and Hawkins of. Evidence? Planted in his flat while he was working. Lots of it. Molloy was now a civilian like the rest of us. We drank to that.

"The tie-in with Jake," Molloy said, "is that Jake stumbled on one of their gatherings. It seems one of Louie's clients" (Dan gazed into the fireplace at this point in the story) "had a fetish for dressing up in Nazi uniform, the genuine article, which he brought with him on his visits. Louie's role was to play a naked victim begging for mercy." I shuddered at the thought. Dan's eyes were glazed. "Sorry about this," Molloy said, suddenly aware of the tension. "Anyway, the end result was that Louie had to beat him with his jackboots. So Jake, bored of being watchdog one night, decided to follow this fellow. Tom was with him. They ended up at a house in Sutton Coldfield. A big house with lots of cars arriving. Tom stayed in the car while Jake scouted in the grounds. He saw the whole paraphernalia of swastikas, flags, uniforms, etc., and it scared the shit out of him. He hotfooted it back to the car, unfortunately just as Smith and Hawkins were arriving at the house. They recognised Jake and gave chase, but Tom lost them, being Tom and knowing every corner, cul-de-sac and one-way street for thirty miles around."

Molloy sat back when he'd finished his story. He looked exhausted as he sipped his drink. I suddenly wanted to get out of the city and as far away from the likes of Smith and Hawkins as I could. I could see Dan felt the same.

"Jake's still in danger," Molloy said. "It's only the fact that they knew I was on their backs that's kept them away for a while. And I'm certain they're not finished with me either. They've got some bigwigs in their pissy group. Must have, otherwise I wouldn't have got the boot. You'd better warn Jake to keep out of sight. If he keeps coming here he'll bring more trouble down on you."

Molloy was bitter and angry. Understandably. He wasn't giving off the smell of defeat though, and when he left I got the distinct impression that he had unfinished business to attend to.

"I'll drive over to Rita's and leave a message for Jake," I said to Dan. "You think Molloy will be all right?"

"He'll go down fighting anyway, that's for sure," Dan replied.

When I drove the car out of the side street and on to the main road, I found Colm sitting outside the pub. Waiting. He leapt up when he saw me and ran over to the car.

"I have to go and give a message to Jake in Wolverhampton," I explained. His face went from bright to dull in an instant.

"Have you been seeing him since you came back?" he demanded, as he clambered into the passenger seat, which was slightly small for a man of his size.

"I've seen him once," I answered truthfully.

"Was that on the morning after the night before?" he asked.

"Something like that," I replied.

I don't know what made me be so brutally honest with him. Perhaps the secret wish that he would turn out to be Prince Charming and I'd better be truthful from the start so as not to be left walking about with only one shoe. It was definitely a mistake.

He didn't get violent or anything like that; he just slumped into silence. I followed suit, not knowing what to say anyway. It's a long journey to Wolverhampton and back in silence. Jake was in when I got there and took the message from Molloy seriously, thank goodness. I had been afraid he might want to be a hero.

"I see the answer-to-every-girl's-dreams has caught up with you," Jake said as I left. Colm was sitting bolt upright, not paying attention to anything around him.

At that point if I'd been forced to choose between Jake and Colm I would have chosen Colm without a moment's hesitation. How wrong can you be? Mortally wrong, God said, and lost to Heaven for ever if you're not careful.

I parked the car close by the pub and got out. Colm remained sitting in the car. I got back in and put my hand on his arm. That's when he got violent. He hit me repeatedly about the face, cursing all the time under his breath. I fought but had no chance of escaping. It only lasted a few minutes but it seemed like a week. He gripped my arms and forced me to look at him.

"It was my understanding that you were a virgin before you went with me. Was I mistaken?" he said.

"And where did you get that idea?" I said. My face was still burning and stinging from the slaps. I was in no mood to pander to him.

"From Deirdre," he said.

"Deirdre?"

"Yes. I was telling her how much I'd always liked the both of you, since I was a child. And she said, 'The whore and the virgin is it?'"

"Are you saying you slept with Deirdre?" I shouted.

"I paid!" he said indignantly.

Sheer rage at the hypocrisy of it all gave me the strength I needed to pull free of his grip and rush into the back entrance of the pub. I bolted the door behind me and leaned against it. I was making a lot of noise, but I couldn't tell whether it was laughter or tears.

I never saw Colm again, but I did get a letter from Breda at a later date informing me that information gleaned from Athlone by Mick led her to suggest I steer clear of him. Better late than never, I suppose.

Should you grieve over the loss of something that never really existed in the first place? In a way I suppose I was mourning the loss of the gleeful and friendly child Colm had once been. I had no idea what had happened in the intervening years to turn him into a frightening, if beautiful, lunatic, but I was sad at the loss, and more than relieved at my lucky escape. Something, some instinct, had warned me to be cautious and it had been right. I would have to learn to listen to it more often.

That was me, said God, always ready to claim a victory. What does the Holy Ghost say about it? I asked. I thought I heard the distant sound of laughter, but I couldn't swear to it.

TWENTY-NINE

I NOTICED THAT Louie was spending less and less time at Deirdre's and more and more time with Dan in the bar. They smiled a lot at each other when their eyes met. Nancy seemed happier too, much more noisy than she'd been before, which seemed to me a healthier situation for a child her age. She'd started bringing school-friends home as well. They, of course, were delighted to be in a pub, even though they were shunted out at opening times. I wondered was there anything in human or Godly law to stop a grandfather turning into a father all of a sudden. If there was, Louie and Dan seemed to pay it no heed. Louie told me June had found another girl to work with her. I asked her what had happened to June's sister. She told me June had no sister, only brothers. Another of Jake's fabrications. Deirdre apparently rarely got out of bed. Her rapist continued to visit her, relieved that his chance of fatherhood had not been lost. It was obscene. I wondered, did his barren wife know the facts of the matter? She couldn't possibly. Could she?

A week exactly after my phonecall to Joan's canteen, I got a card from her saying I was welcome any time. It was Tuesday. I decided to work till the end of the week and travel north on the Saturday. It crossed my mind that I would have to find some way of earning a living up there and all I knew about was pulling pints. I felt a little ripple of excitement at the prospect of moving. New places, new faces. There were memories in Birmingham I'd be happy to leave behind me. For ever.

On Wednesday the headline in the evening paper brought me to a complete standstill in the hallway:

TRIPLE DEATH ENDS POLICE CHASE

Inspector Alan Hawkins and Sergeant Robert Smith were last night found dead after a ten-mile car chase. Their police car crashed into the Rover 90 they were pursuing and turned over several times before plunging into a lake. Both bodies were recovered in the early hours of the morning. The driver of the second car, identity unknown so far, died when his car exploded soon after the collision.

The rest of the report was a eulogy about their character and reputation in the police force and details of their families left behind. Robert Smith was a bachelor still living with his parents. Hawkins left behind a widow and two teenage sons. I read the first part again. Molloy had always driven an old Rover 90 when he wasn't on duty.

I called Dan. He read the article and then did some phoning around. No sign of Molloy in the usual haunts. That evening, every time the bar door opened, our eyes prayed for Molloy to walk in. He didn't. Jake did. He'd read the report as well. That made three of us watching the door. No luck.

At intervals during the evening my mind felt almost unhinged. More deaths, and all I could think of was whether Molloy had survived. God had every reason for abandoning me, I was a lost cause. I seemed to be able to adapt to the most awful situations and show concern only for those I cared about. What about the rest of humanity? Could I really feel so detached or was I kidding myself, suppressing all the difficult bits, determined that I would cope, no matter what? There really was a lot of similarity between me and Deirdre. When you got down to it, we were both selfish. Parental fault? Genetic problem? Loss of God? Who knows? I do, God said. I wasn't prepared to listen.

I thought again about running away to Yorkshire. Was it just escape? Did I actually want to change? Could I do that by turning my back on difficult and uncomfortable situations? And who could ever trust a God who never seemed to be around when He was needed and who allowed all sorts of atrocities to be committed all over the world in His name. Freedom of choice is what I gave when I died on the cross, He said angrily.

At closing time we were all gloomy. Jake asked if he could stay in the snug. I protested, but he said he only wanted to save himself a trip back to Wolverhampton. Once a liar, always a liar. Fortunately I discovered I was made of sterner stuff. I resisted. It was against his principles to insist. We ended up laughing helplessly at three in the morning as we tried to get to sleep without touching one another. In the end we cuddled like two spoons and slept well.

By Friday morning there was still no word of Molloy. Dan and I prepared ourselves to accept the obvious conclusion and set about finding out where the unknown corpse was to be buried. Dan had his coat on ready to visit the mortuary when a telegram arrived. It was from Ireland. It said:

> Renewing my acquaintance with uncle.
> God, isn't confession a great thing!
> Molloy

Years later we found out that the unidentified body had belonged to the ex-major in the British army who Molloy had kidnapped and used as bait. Things had turned out better than he'd planned. He swears it was the hand of God which intervened. I think staying with Father Molloy for two years twisted his mind. Last I heard of him he was running a bar in Cashel.

Should I have felt horror at Molloy luring three men to their deaths? Mostly I felt relief that Molloy had survived when the odds had been stacked against him. Was it that I needed to bury and repress any "normal" response in order to avoid facing my own complicity in murder?

What was a normal reaction anyway? What God said? All I knew for sure was that I wanted strong feelings. I wanted passion and I was prepared to take the consequences.

You will, God said, on the Day of Judgement.

Friday evening I had everything packed ready for my departure. It had been arranged that everyone would come to the pub that evening to give me a rousing send-off. Deirdre phoned at seven to say she wouldn't be coming. In spite of everything I couldn't bring myself to leave without seeing her.

The flat was in darkness when I got there. No sign of

June or friend. Deirdre shuffled to the door in an old brown-checked dressing-gown which must have belonged to a fifteen-stone man before her. It reached across the lump. Just. She looked tired out. I couldn't believe she slept all the time; it looked more like she hadn't slept for several weeks. There were dark rings under her eyes and the eyes themselves were badly bloodshot.

"Oh, it's you," she said. Full of interest as usual. I followed her into her bedroom, watching her slippered feet slop-slopping like an old woman's. She was wearing grey men's socks, which were hanging over the side of the slippers. Getting back into bed seemed like a major operation but she managed it eventually. I didn't try to help, having got so used to her snubs.

"You don't look well," I said.

"Stating the obvious as usual, I see," she responded.

"Is there anything I can get for you?"

"Some tranquillisers for this bugger in here," she said pointing at her stomach. "It never keeps still from morning till night."

I avoided making any comments about the baby. I had learned something about Deirdre's reactions, even though I'd only seen her rarely over the past few months.

"Louie all right?" she asked.

"Great, it seems." Don't use three words when two will do, I warned myself. Deirdre stared at the ceiling.

"I'll miss you," I blurted out into the gap in conversation.

She looked at me as if I were aiming a gun at her head, then she lifted her mouth up at the corner. It could have been a smile but I didn't want to bank on it.

"Miss me?" She croaked. "You must be joking. Nobody

would miss me if I bumped myself off tomorrow. Oh, Mam and Dad maybe, but then they don't know me like you do, do they, Bernie?" I think she smiled again.

I let the silence grow for a while. At least I hadn't been told to leave; that had to be an advance.

"Can I be with you for the birth?" I tried. I'd been wanting to ask for weeks.

"What for? So that you can gloat over the pain?"

"Just in case you need me. I've read that women get strange feelings when they're giving birth."

She sighed, long and slow. It reminded me of the noise the old goat used to make back home.

"I'm not giving birth, Bernie," she said. "I'm expelling an unwanted parasite!"

"So, can I be here for the expulsion?"

"Sure, I suppose, the more the merrier. You can have the job of wiping my bottom." She stared at me, willing me to react.

I fought down the urge to shout. I struggled with the bile rising in my throat. I knew she wanted to hurt me like she'd been hurt. She felt disgusted with herself and she wanted everyone to feel the same about her. I left Joan's work telephone number by the bedside clock and kissed her on the cheek. She turned her head away from me. As I moved to go she grabbed hold of my hand and squeezed it, but she wouldn't look at me.

"You're a big girl now, Bernie," she said. "You can stop blaming Mam and Dad for everything that's wrong with you. Go out and make something of your life, grab it with both hands. You're the survivor. Remember?" I cried all the way back to the pub.

There had been race riots in Notting Hill that week. Dan had warned that the "Irish question" would be brought to England again before too long. He pointed out one of the old pub stalwarts, Jonjo McGrath, and told me he'd been involved with *The Irish Workers' Voice*, fought with the International Brigade in Spain and would die fighting "for the cause".

There's hundreds like him over here," Dan said. "The injustice of it all is branded on their brains. Mark my words."

As we were clearing up after closing time I took hold of Dan's hands. "I'll miss you, Dan," I managed to say before the tears began again. He held me for a long time, until I felt pressed dry of emotion.

"There'll always be a job here for you," he said. "Come back whenever you want."

"If things had been different I could have loved you," I said.

"You would have been easy to love," he replied. It wasn't what I'd expected him to say. "But I'm not the right one for you."

"Is he out there somewhere, do you think?"

"He is, without a doubt, and you'll know him when you meet him. There'll be no confusion."

THIRTY

I GOT DRUNK as a bluebell in a storm on Friday night and had to be carried into the snug completely legless. Faces swam in and out and around as I travelled that choppy ocean of over-indulgence: people wishing me well; asking me questions; demanding answers to questions they'd never asked me; making me promise things I didn't approve of. I was sick several times in the night into the conveniently placed bucket which Louie had thoughtfully provided. As going away parties go, I'd say it was pretty fair.

Dan promised he wouldn't pass on my address to anyone without first checking with me. I was thinking of Colm, I suppose, but it doesn't cost anything to be careful. Jake said he would keep an eye on Deirdre. He had more time to spare, as he'd been sacked from the Wolverhampton job after being found in bed with a female patient. The woman had defended him, saying she'd been terrified about an operation she was to have the next day. Hysterectomy. She'd been feeling old and unattractive and sexually dead. Jake had given her a new lease of life and she'd had the surgery with a lighter heart. However, the hospital administration had rules to uphold. He was banished. Rita gave him the boot as well. She'd taken up with a rugby player who she'd nursed back to health. He loved competition it seems, as long as it wasn't connected with bed.

I took off early Saturday morning in Tom's car with everyone's blessing. The sun was shining, so I took it that He approved of my new direction in life as well. I still wasn't fully legal, so I hoped that the police in the other counties I had to pass through were as indulgent as the ones in Birmingham. I couldn't very well produce Tom O'Neill's driving licence if I was stopped, although it was fine for insurance purposes.

I got lost, inevitably, within three miles of Joan's house and had some difficulty understanding the directions helpful strangers gave me. I don't know whether it was the accents or not. I ended up in the pit yard on one of my attempts and found that in fact it was the easiest way to approach her house. She lived in a square of terraces with a large green in the middle of it. You could see the pit winding-gear from her front garden. There were outside lavatories shared by adjoining houses, which reminded me a little of home, though they weren't as primitive as ours. They did have a flush and a proper seat.

Joan had a huge dinner of sausage, mashed potatoes, peas and carrots waiting for me, with rice pudding to follow. She took me in her arms as soon as she saw me and I smelled Evening in Paris perfume! Would I never escape from it?

Joan had redecorated her spare bedroom especially for me. It was mostly yellow with the odd touch of green. It looked fresh and inviting and made me feel young.

"I did it when I got back from Scarborough," Joan said. "Thought it would make it feel really like your room. Of course, you've got the run of the house, love, but everyone needs a quiet spot to call their own, eh?"

After dinner she took me to the local shops, a long string of them all on one side of the Great North Road, starting with a little sweetshop next to the picture house and ending with a little sweetshop next to the park. She pointed out the best places to shop, the hairdresser's she went to once a week, the bookie's, in case I liked a little flutter, and the place to spend the Provident cheques.

"Although your best bet is Bon Marché in town," she said. "They get all the really modern stuff in. We'll go in on Monday when I finish work. There's a bowling alley just opened up and I've been dying to have a go. You can get food in there as well, just like on the films."

She bought me Veet cream hair remover to "get rid of the wire wool" on my legs, some Amami Henna brilliantine to highlight my hair and an Excelsior bra to give me "better uplift". I felt as if I was being taken in hand, and perhaps it wasn't before time.

Joan listened to the "Light Programme" on the radio while I unpacked and settled into my little nest. That's what it seemed like, with all the leaves and flowers on the walls, bed and curtains. Even on the carpet. I could hear her through the floor joining in with some of the songs on the radio. I lay on top of the bed and decided that I was pleased with the move, even though there were a number of question marks over the future. Joan woke me up about an hour later as she tried to tuck me under the covers.

She was going out for the day with Jack on the Sunday. "But there's plenty of food in the pantry, so don't go short," she said, handing me a key to the back door. "There's an old road atlas in the sideboard drawer if you want to have a drive about. It's not all slag heaps and pitheads, you know; there's some lovely countryside."

I didn't get to meet Jack, just heard the delicate parp of the car hooter when he arrived. "He's a bit shy, y'know," Joan said. Then she roared with laughter and rushed off in a cloud of Max Factor face powder.

Joan was right about the countryside. It was attractive. It changed from flat fields with sparse trees to rolling hills and woods to wild moorland in a matter of miles. I drove along a river for some of the way and enjoyed following its twists and turns. It reminded me of the land around Breda and Mick's house at home.

It was a beautiful bright day, with a light wind and the scent of freshly cut grass.

Back in the shadow of the winding-gear I sat on the doorstep and watched the comings and goings of my new world. A small knot of young miners came along with a sense of determination in their step. They nodded, winked and smiled at me as they knocked on Joan's neighbour's door. A woman in her early forties opened it and blocked it with her large frame, arms folded high on her bolster-like breasts.

"We've come for Derek," one of the men said.

"He's not coming," came her swift reply. From somewhere inside the house a man's voice called to "wait up". It was a stand-off! The woman didn't budge; the men waited. Then through the middle of them came two young women carrying a wind-up gramophone. They were a year or two older than me and dressed more fashionably. They flirted and chattered with the men as they set up the gramophone on the ground. When they saw me they smiled and walked over.

"You must be Bernie," the darker one said. "I'm Molly and this is my sis, Maria." She giggled. "Can you sing?"

"Not very well," I replied.

"Can you dance?" Maria asked, indicating the gramophone. "We're going to jitterbug about. Is that what it's called, Moll?"

"That's what Tommy said. He's our big brother, working down in London with a band."

The quiet stand-off next door suddenly erupted into an argument. A young man, Derek I presumed, tried to leave the house. The woman tried to block his way. "Get back inside, Derek. I'll not have you led astray by these troublemakers," she said.

"Give over, Mam. I've told yer, I'm going and that's it."

Molly dug me gently in the ribs and grinned. "That's our Derek trying to break free of Mum's apron strings. She's tightened them even more since Tommy went down south."

"They're off to a mass meeting," Maria said. "Coal Board's gonna close down a load of pits in the next six years. Lads are protesting."

Molly and Maria Peters got me dancing in the street. After a while Mrs Peters came out and joined in. Eventually there was quite a crowd. Someone made a tray of tea, someone else brought fish-paste sandwiches and Mrs Peters fetched out a tray of freshly baked buns.

I found out that Molly was a bus conductress with Yorkshire Traction. She was very proud of her smart brown uniform. The click-click of her heels as she strode out to work each morning was like an alarm clock, seven-fifteen on the dot. Maria was a hairdresser and decided within minutes that my thatch needed taking in hand.

I met Sandra, a ten-year-old polio sufferer who had a hug like a grizzly bear and guarded the square like a lion. Her speech was slurred and loud, her legs were in calipers, but her smile cheered up the dimmest day.

The strangest phenomenon I observed that day was the total acceptance of me as an individual but, in almost the same breath, a quiet hostility to all the foreigners coming into the country. One of the main spokesmen for the protesting miners was an Irishman, Kevin O'Mara. In fact, I discovered, the very same man who'd been sending books to Dan all those years. He wasn't the most popular of figures with Mrs Peters and some of the others, but I was determined to meet him. By the time Joan got back I was exhausted.

— THIRTY-ONE —

"**D**ID YOU HAVE a good time?" I asked, as we sat watching the fire with a pot of tea brewing close by.

"Yes, love, always do with Jack. We went to York, had a walk round and then dinner in a pub. Nice place, York."

The tea was strong and refreshing. I lit up a Woodbine. No sickness any more. I'd done my smoking apprenticeship. Joan smoked Park Drive. If our lungs protested we couldn't hear them above the noise of the radio.

"Do you ever think about Jack's wife?" I asked. "You know, ever feel guilty?"

"No, love," she said. "In fact I think it's probably done their marriage the world of good, him having this thing with me. He's more considerate to her than he ever was before. I've seen to that. He remembers birthdays, buys her flowers. Yes, I'm sure she's a lot better off, and Jack says she was never much interested in sex after she'd had the children. Didn't see the point. Some women are like that, you know. It's all right while the kids are being produced, but when they've got the family they want sex goes out the window." She was laughing as she arranged biscuits on a flowered plate. Perhaps remembering something her and Jack had been up to earlier in the day. I felt a twinge of jealousy. It all seemed so straightforward to Joan.

"What about you then?" I asked. "You've not had any kids have you?"

Her face went into shadow and then out again, almost
in the blink of an eye. Things weren't quite so simple then.

"We tried," she said somewhat sadly. "I had three mis-
carriages. Doctors said we might as well give up then, my
insides were in such a mess. I was all ready to adopt, but
Ted didn't want that; said he only wanted his own kids,
own blood and all that. I think that's the main reason he's
with someone younger than me. She has no problems with
her insides as far as anyone knows."

"Are you sorry?"

"About him being with someone else? I suppose so in
a way, but I've gotten used to the idea now." She leant over
and patted my knee. "You can be the one I never had."

That did it. A person can only take so much affection
after being starved of it for years. The lid flew off the well
and it all started pouring out. Joan's face went through as
many permutations of emotions as you can imagine.
Another pot of tea was made during the outpouring.
Most of the time I stared into the fire while I was talking,
adding lumps of coal and bits of wood when necessary.

Joan was silent for some time after I'd finished. I felt
totally drained so I didn't mind sitting back and absorb-
ing the quiet. The radio was off, the lights weren't on and
it was dark in the room except for the glow of the fire.
Joan's body made huge shadows on the wall as she stirred
in her seat.

"Whoever said we would automatically love our own
flesh and blood? If you'd seen what I've seen, you'd doubt
it as much as me, Bernie. Maybe your mam was able to
be more honest than most, duck. Have you thought of
that? After what she went through you must have been

like a constant reminder. You probably look like him. I've seen mams and dads who were supposed to love their kids treat them horribly: beatings, locking 'em up in cupboards, humiliation, all sorts. Some stuff you wouldn't believe if I told you." She watched me for a second before continuing. "And Deirdre is right, in a way," she continued.

"What way?" I snapped. The last thing I wanted was Deirdre pushing her way into my new life.

"We all have to grow up, take responsibility, stop blaming our parents every time something goes wrong for us. Don't we?"

I didn't reply. The truth often hurts.

"And besides," she said softly, "we can grow to really love people who aren't family and that love is freely given, not bound by duty and such like."

"You're a wise old bird, aren't you, Joan," I said at last.

"Less of the old, if you don't mind," she laughed.

Joan was away to work by the time I got up. She'd left a note propped on the teapot. "I'll be back at 3pm or come up to the canteen before if you'd like. Anyone will tell you the way. Help yourself to anything you want."

I walked up the lane to the pithead. I could see the canteen with its steamed-up windows suggesting hot food, mugs of tea and lots of cigarette smoke. Discarded placards and other remnants of yesterday's protest were stacked by the wall. I took myself down to the shops and gazed in an unfocused way at what was on offer. I found two pubs, the Bay Horse and the Moon, where I enquired after work. Nothing doing.

"There's things need our attention," I said to Joan the next day, "like me finding a way of earning a living. I'm not going to take advantage of you."

"I'll take you into town later today when I get back from work and show you where the unemployment place and everything is," Joan said.

I got up and cleared the kitchen after she left for work, then walked down to the ribbon of shops. Cold, damp day, making everyone look low and down at the mouth. Me too. I bought myself a bar of chocolate. Compensation. I ate it in the park, swinging gently on one of the swings. Up and down, up and down, an imitation of life. There were a few children on the other swings, anxious mothers keeping half an eye on them while they caught up on gossip.

I wandered up towards the pit yard and down a lane which led to a small wood. Only a tiny stretch of greenery among the slag heaps, but enough to hide in. To sit and think. Time to forget about the past and look towards the future.

It was almost dinnertime when I got back to Joan's, none the wiser but a great deal colder. Count your blessings, God said. There was a note propped up on the table in front of the sugar bowl. It said, "Ring Birmingham. Urgent." Joan must have been back while I was out. I grabbed my purse and rushed out to the public phone booth. Dan answered on the second ring.

"Yes?" he said. When I heard his voice I felt as if I'd been gone from the pub for years.

"It's Bernie," I said. "I got a message to ring."

"Oh Bernie," he sighed. "Thank goodness. Deirdre has gone into labour and she keeps asking for you, saying she promised. Can you come?"

"I'm leaving now," I said. I was just about to put the phone down when I heard Dan shouting down the receiver.

"Bernie!" he said. "She's at the pub here. We fetched her over because of the phone, you know, in case we have to get her to the hospital."

I knew. I also knew that the filthy rapist would have been informed and that he'd be waiting to get his hands on the fresh, new child. I was shuddering at the thought all the time I threw stuff into my bag, all the way to the car, and in fact most of the journey. A voice, not God's, kept saying, "Mind your own business." I didn't want to listen to it but I couldn't see any alternative. I drove fast and dangerously, foolish in my haste to get there, my concentration not on the road but on images in my head and conflicting thoughts and emotions about myself and Deirdre. The past was forcing its way back into my mind, determined I shouldn't ignore it. I realised as I reached the outskirts of the city that I was hungry. Only the chocolate since breakfast. It was just after four when I arrived at the pub. Cheese and onion sandwich, I thought, but when I walked into Dan's bedroom and saw Deirdre all thoughts of food disappeared.

She looked just like a wild animal. Her hair stood out in all directions, as if the rats had been sucking at it. Her face was alternately flushed then pale as the contractions came and went. Two minutes; ninety seconds; one minute between them. Sweat shone on every exposed part of her body. Louie and Rita stood at either side of the bed. Deirdre shifted about, changing position constantly. In the bar Jake and Dan sat bent over their drinks, wanting to be a million miles away. If anything, they looked in a worse state than Deirdre. Hunched, drawn, haggard looking. Perhaps the first birth they'd been around for. God, of course, had presided at many. Multitudes, He said smugly.

I arrived in the room in the middle of a contraction. Every time Deirdre took a breath or began to pant, it seemed like everyone else joined in. It was as if the whole room were a giant womb, pulsating, roaring with energy. I felt exhilarated by it, the beginning of a new life, the miracle of birth. But the men, what did they feel? At least I had the ability to give birth one day if I chose to, but not them. Is that what they were feeling? A loss? An exclusion? Fear? We were back at the start of it all; primeval sounds issued from Deirdre's swollen lips; the infant animal was pushing its way out into the world; nothing would stop it. Insistent. Determined. Self-centred. And we'd all been there once. We all came slurping out of our mothers' bodies, hot, shivering, lardy, desperate for love.

Louie moved to one side so that Deirdre could see me. She smiled, bared her teeth really, for the pains were almost continuous. I started stroking her back, shoulders, neck. She nodded, letting me know it felt good. I saw the fierceness of her grip on Louie's hand; her total absorption in the process she was going through.

"I can see the head," Rita said suddenly. "Look," she said to everyone in the room. Louie looked then went back to her position. I stayed on, fascinated. Could that be a head?

"You'll have to push when I tell you now, Deirdre," Rita said. "Okay, now hold it, just hold it, now, gently, gently. That's it. Stop now."

And so it went on. Deirdre now on all fours gripping the top of the bed.

"It's coming. Just one more gentle push, that's it, gently."

And there it was! I nearly passed out with shock when the head appeared fully. The baby's eyes blinked as soon as it emerged. I was staggered. Then all of a sudden there was a whoosh and the whole body lay there between Deirdre's legs. There were tears running down my cheeks as Rita handed me the little bundle to hold while she snipped the umbilical cord. I could hear Deirdre's voice saying, "Take it away! Take it away!" but the words weren't registering.

Rita brought me back to earth when she took the baby out of my arms, wrapped it in a couple of blankets and put it in the wicker basket Louie was holding.

"*Take it away!*" Deirdre screamed again, and before I could even swallow Louie was leaving the room carrying the basket. Jake sat in the hallway with his head in his hands, taking deep breaths to try and stop the vomit. He failed. Rita threw a cloth and a look of disgust in his direction and continued cleaning Deirdre and making her comfortable. I went to kiss her, but she was already asleep.

"Probably sleep for a few hours now," Rita said. "She needs it. Why don't you have a rest too? I have to go on duty at nine, so you'll be needed then."

Rest! I felt as wound up as a ball of wool and ready to unravel at any minute. The baby had been a boy, and I'd seen a small, crescent-shaped birthmark on his forehead as Rita took him from me. Somehow, the fact that it was a boy lessened my fright at the rapist getting his hands on it. I felt a boy would be less vulnerable, but still I wasn't happy. I shot down the pub stairs and out of the backyard in time to see Louie, Dan and the bundle getting into a taxi.

I didn't understand why I was following them and at that moment I didn't care. It was something I felt compelled to do. At that startling moment of birth, when the child had opened his eyes and looked at me, a link had been created between us.

— THIRTY-TWO —

A S I FOLLOWED the taxi through its twists and turns,
unaware of just where we were headed, I suddenly
realised why Jake was in such a bad way. He'd been on
the fringes of this pregnancy right from the start, watched
Deirdre grow and suffer, and now seen the pain of child-
birth. Particularly painful when it's unwanted. It must
have made him think back to the time she had given birth
to his baby. Even though he hadn't been there, hadn't
known about it until after the event, so he said, maybe
he'd never really thought about it in terms of the reality
of birth. Or was it more than that? Was it the realisation
that he'd once been there, small, vulnerable, helpless?
Totally dependent on the woman who was his mother.

The taxi pulled into a tree-lined drive and stopped. I
parked and got out of the car. We were somewhere in
Solihull. I saw Dan and Louie hurry into the entrance of
an old Victorian house. The sign at the entrance indicated
that it was a private nursing home. Was Mrs Rapist
sitting up in bed in there in her flowered nightie waiting
to take delivery? Could I blame her? Maybe she was
desperate for a child, unable to have her own. Maybe she
would be a kind mother despite her husband. Maybe.
Whosoever shall harm one of these little ones, God said.
Sod off! I said to Him. What about all the children who
have suffered and died on this earth? Why didn't You lift

a finger to help them? Fear of the Lord? I think not.

Dan and Louie were back out in a matter of minutes. I hid amongst the trees and watched them drive past. Louie had her head on Dan's shoulder, he was comforting her. Can't have been an easy thing to do. I couldn't have done it. Of course, that's why Deirdre didn't ask me. I crept up to the glass porch. I could see a woman in a nurse's uniform at the reception desk writing in a book. A baby cried out from along the corridor. Was it him? The nurse went clip-clopping in the direction of the sound. I nipped in quickly and looked at the book. There were only a few patients in and only one who had freshly written by her name: "Baby arrived 8pm." I looked at my watch having lost all sense of time. Just a few minutes past eight. The woman's name was Mrs Mellor, the address at the posh end of Solihull. The number of her room was there too, 4G.

I left undetected and sat in my car for about ten minutes. The thoughts that were forming were frightening, unasked for, surely a form of madness brought on by the birth. You could take the baby, the voice in my head said; you could bring it up. It wasn't God. He's always far more practical than that. I pushed the suggestion away roughly and started the car. At the end of the street I paused to check the name of the road, just in case I needed to come back?

The bar was open when I returned. Jake was propping it up. Louie had gone to pick up Nancy from a friend's house and Dan looked as if he'd been turned into a pillar of salt. Upstairs Rita was packing up her things, ready to go on duty. I offered her a lift but she smiled and said her man was on his way. Deirdre slept on, her hair forming damp ringlets on the pillow. I sat for an hour just watching her sleep, remembering the child she'd been at her first birth, the woman she was now. Was there a connecting thread between the two events? Was it sheer lunacy even to contemplate raising a child on my own? I didn't even have a job and only a roof over my head by courtesy of Joan. Jake appeared in the doorway looking tired and anxious.

"That woman Joan is on the phone for you," he said quietly. "I'll sit with Deirdre for a bit." This was not the Jake I knew. Something had snapped within him. His eyes, looking at Deirdre, were wary. All sign of mischief was gone. I squeezed his hand as I passed him. He nodded absently in response.

I explained to Joan about the evening's events, including my own mad thoughts. She was a good listener. "So your head and your heart are telling you two different things?" she said. I agreed. "I've always found the heart to be a very untrustworthy ally. It usually gets you into trouble. But its motivations are always better than those the head would have you follow. I know that's not much help, but in the end it all comes down to you. Anyway, love, I was just wondering when you might be coming back?"

"I'll probably stay until next weekend, make sure Deirdre's all right and maybe earn a few bob in the process," I said.

"Well there's been a bit of a crisis here. The old man's latest girlfriend has gone and left him, and I think he might be heading here, trying to wheedle his way back in with me. I've worked it all out with the boss at work so that I can skip off for a few days, keeping out of the way. So I'll see you next weekend, love."

"Okay, Joan," I said. "And thanks."

"Are you sure you're going to be all right? Only I could pop down if you like."

"I'll be fine. The body's willing, it's the head that's weak."

"See you then," she finished. "Oh, and don't forget there are three bedrooms in my house, if you should decide to bring a friend back."

"Joan, are you saying what I think you're saying?" I asked tentatively.

"What d'you think?" she responded.

"We could end up in prison."

"All part of life's rich tapestry. Do what you have to do, Bernie. I'll be right behind you. Okay?"

"Thanks. I'll see you soon."

So, she could read me like a map; had patched together all the fragments of what I'd told her; had sensed the struggle that was going on inside me.

I crept back upstairs to check on Deirdre. Jake was lying on the bed with her, wrapped around her like a scarf. They were both asleep. With a tiny start I realised for the first time how well matched they looked, how they seemed to fit together.

The snug welcomed me with open-armed familiarity. I was so exhausted from the journey, the nervous energy of the birth and the thoughts that had been circling for hours that I fell asleep instantly.

Deirdre was sitting up in bed next morning looking rested but still weak. Jake had brought her breakfast in bed. She didn't want to eat anything, but Jake was insisting. Deirdre made a face at him, screwing up her eyes and putting out her tongue. I hadn't seen her do it for the best part of ten years. The shadow that had been her face ever since I'd arrived in England was gone, but not her animosity towards me.

"You came then," she said coldly to me.

"Yes. Thanks for letting me know."

"And I suppose it was a wonderful experience for you," she said. I didn't reply. "Yes, it would have been, wouldn't it?" she went on. "You seem to thrive on other people's misery. Why don't you just piss off and get on with your life and leave me alone?"

Jake was stroking her hands, trying to calm her down, not very effectively.

"Perhaps you'd better stay out of the way for a bit," he said to me. Deirdre looked triumphant at Jake coming down firmly on her side at last. I left the room. No point inviting insults. Besides, it was true. It had been a great experience for me, but I didn't think the thrill would last. Good things rarely seem to. Maybe that was the motive behind wanting the baby. That was something that would last. A whole lifetime. I will be here for Eternity, God chipped in. One lifetime will do for me, I replied peevishly.

I drove out to the nursing home and parked opposite the entrance. I don't know what I thought I was going to do. Just walk in and take the baby? Demand it be given to me because it was my sister's? They'd have the police around without a second thought. Wouldn't they? Only my word against theirs, after all. And who was I? Some upstart Irish tart.

I went to the nursing home every day until Friday just to sit and watch. I worked and nattered to Dan and Louie in between times, but Deirdre still had the "keep out" sign up on her door as far as I was concerned. Jake was with her constantly. He seemed to be regaining his health along with her. I felt cut off from these couples. Dan and Louie did their best to make me feel welcome, but there's just no way you can penetrate them, not while things are going well anyway. I longed for Joan. At least her forays with Jack were limited, not all-embracing, not intimidating. Not saying to me: what's wrong with you? Why aren't you part of a couple?

Friday afternoon I went shopping. I bought Ostermilk powder, nappies, cream, talcum powder, a few clothes and books on babies. I took a soft blanket from Dan's and made a bed with it on the back seat of the car. I put a pillow case inside it for the baby's sheets. I had just enough money left for my petrol back to Yorkshire when I'd finished. I felt pleased to feel so confident now that I'd reached a decision. I would have to steal the baby. There was no other way.

Deirdre came down in the bar while I was working on Friday evening. It was heaving with bodies. While I rushed up and down serving drinks and generally making myself useful, she sat watching me, not saying a word. Jake hovered beside her. When Dan called "time" she caught me by the arm and whispered in my ear.

"Just wanted you to know, Miss Goody Goody," she said. "The money I got for the baby, I tore it up and burnt it!" Jake nodded, indicating the truth of what she said. Jake kissed her and squeezed her hand. She dropped her head on to his shoulder affectionately.

Deirdre and Jake seemed to have really found one another at last. That long-ago meeting of bodies behind the tinkers' camp had stretched between them like fibre, knotting and twisting them together. I was glad. I wanted them to be happy. I knew that Jake could pull Deirdre out of the swamp if he really wanted to. When I caught him alone outside the snug I told him so.

"Take her home, Jake. This life will kill her if you don't. Mam and Dad will leave the cottage to Deirdre, you'd have a bit of land . . ."

He interrupted me by putting his finger on my lips.

"We'll do what we do, Bernie, just like you," he said. "And I'll still love you, even if you do go in for kidnapping."

I opened my mouth to protest but knew from the look in those familiar eyes that he'd been following me. No point in denial.

"I'll look after Deirdre, don't you worry," he said, "and keep in touch, because she does care about you underneath all that bravado."

He kissed me before returning to the bar, Deirdre and his future. It was the sweetest kiss I'd ever had from him.

— THIRTY-THREE —

M Y PLANNING GOT me as far as the step outside the nursing home. It was nearly midnight, Friday night. If all went well I would be heading north in no time at all, arriving at Joan's in the early hours. The trouble was, I'd no idea how I was going to get in and out of the damned place, let alone abduct the baby, without all hell being let loose. I moved back into the trees and waited. Maybe inspiration would hit if I gave it an opportunity. Perhaps an ambulance would arrive with an emergency patient. Did that sort of thing happen in private nursing homes? I had no idea. One o'clock came and went and still nothing. I was stiff and aching. Unwanted thoughts had been rooting round inside my brain for some time, winding me up, poking at me. Human relationships, loyalty, love: what did they all come down to? Ashes to ashes, God said. He never knew when to stop.

Then I saw it, a flicker of movement at the side of the house. The scene was easily interpreted. A nurse and her bloke, giggling and kissing, finding it hard to tear themselves apart. Now she was half walking, half being led by him towards the back entrance to the garden. I'd been round there several times already. A little snicket led to a side street round the corner. Once they were out of sight I ran like mad and entered the house by the door they'd left on the latch. First things first. I headed for the front door, drew back the bolts and opened it, wedging it a tiny bit apart with a matchbox. I heard the nurse returning just as I finished. I dropped down on to my knees and held the inner door closed in case it caused a draught.

The nurse seemed to be doing a round of the patients. I could hear doors being opened and shut with care. That was good, probably meant she would go and have a sleep. Dream about her boyfriend. I waited for about ten minutes after she'd disappeared up a stairway. Nothing. Except of course the thunder of blood in my ears and the throb of my heart. I felt suddenly very scared. Panic made my feet into iron plates. I took deep breaths for a few seconds, checked my escape route, and walked softly down the corridor looking at the door numbers. 8G, 7G, 6G, 5G, 4G. I put my ear to the door. Not a sound. I prayed the door wouldn't squeak or creak when I started to open it. It didn't.

I closed the door quietly behind me and stood stock still, barely breathing, for almost two minutes. Once my eyes had adjusted to the dark, I could see that the baby lay in a hospital cot, plastic, see-through, clinical. The woman was turned away from me and the baby and sleeping soundly. I was surprised that the thudding of my heart didn't wake her.

That was the moment when I suddenly realised the full implication of what I was planning. Stealing a baby and bringing it up as my own. My sister's baby, born out of rape. God, are You watching me now, I thought. Yes, He replied. Who do you think got you into this position in the first place? Are you claiming rape as one of Your acts of goodness? I asked. That was Satan's work, He replied.

The future of the baby is My concern . . . and yours.

Am I being supported by You in this act of abduction then? I thought "Thou shalt not steal" was one of the Big Ten? It's all down to interpretation, Bernadette. All that stuff in the bible was written years ago and years after the event.

Which event?

The death of My son.

For a minute there He sounded almost human. I dug my nails into the palms of my hands to bring me to my senses. This was not the time or the place to be having a conversation with an imaginary being.

I felt ill with fear. I knew the longer I waited the more danger there was of being caught. The baby or the woman might wake at any second. The nurse could walk in. The front door might be discovered to be open. I also knew that if I hesitated much more I wouldn't be able to go through with it.

I surveyed the room quickly. There was a bottle of milk made up on the bedside table. I put it into my pocket. The baby's medical chart was clipped to the cot; it might hold valuable information. I removed it from the clipboard. It rustled faintly.

The woman stirred and moaned a little in her sleep. I froze. The baby gave a soft mew. I took a deep breath, bent down and lifted him up. I pressed him close to my chest, rocking him ever so slightly. In the light from the moon I saw the crescent-shaped birthmark. I smelled cinnamon, lemon, a musky sweetness. I felt breathless.

Outside the room the corridor was empty and silent. It seemed a mile to the front door. The baby wriggled a

little, mewed, grunted. I made the most heartfelt plea I'd
ever made in my entire life.

Please, God, let me get out of here safely.

What's it worth? He replied.

Stuff you, I responded. I began the long walk. Upstairs
a door opened and footsteps sounded.

See! He said.

I won't go back to the Church but I will reconsider my
opinion of You, I said.

My head was on fire. The footsteps echoed away from
the top of the stairs, another door opened and closed. I
moved quickly and silently. Seconds later I had the door
open. Cool air wafted against my feverish face. I shut the
door quietly.

I lay the baby on its bed on the back seat and relaxed
a little. Still a long way to go. The car started first time.
Driving away from Birmingham took me through many
twists and turns of memory. I wondered how far fate had
determined it all.

If by fate you mean Me, God said, then I've been in it
right from the start. He was gaining in confidence again,
I'd have to be careful.

On the motorway I felt twinges of anxiety, but the
purple night sky and the twinkling of headlights seemed
to lead me on. I began to go over everything, in as much
detail as I could, from the moment I first saw Jake. The
connections back through Isobel, May, Grandad Joseph,
the potential ways forward. And some of the reasons why
God and I had never really hit it off. Maybe it was the
heightened sense of reality; the fear about what I'd done;
the desperate need to understand. Whatever, by the time

I'd reached present time I was driving through a small town called Ripley in Derbyshire and heading for the A1. That was when baby started to cry.

I stopped the car by a lake near a large ironworks. My whole body seemed to be in spasm. The shaking was so violent that the car rocked. Miraculously, baby stopped crying and made little grunting noises instead.

Miraculous is the right word, God said.

I paused before answering. What I had to say was far too important to rush.

Let me speak to Your mother, I said eventually as my shivering subsided.

Don't be ridiculous, He said, but I could hear fear gurgling in His throat.

The baby started whimpering.

I want to talk to the Mother of God, I said. She's the only one who can help me now.

His voice was petulant when He replied.

You promised to re-evaluate, He said.

The baby's whimpering grew louder. It looked so small and helpless and new and beautiful.

Well? He said, desperate to regain the upper hand.

Put the Holy Ghost on then, I responded. I need the help of an experienced woman.

Silence. And He remained silent for the rest of the journey. Baby quietened down when I picked him up. Eyes which I knew couldn't see seemed to look right into me, seemed to understand everything. I felt an outpouring of love. It enveloped me. It gave me momentum.

Baby wasn't too happy that the milk was cold. He spat out the first few mouthfuls in disgust, but when I started singing softly he settled to the teat with a vengeance. I promised him there and then that, if the law didn't catch up with us or, worse still, Deirdre, he would get more love than any child had ever had.

—THIRTY-FOUR—

JOAN TOOK TO the role of surrogate grandma very easily, though none of us had a proper night's sleep for months. Nothing appeared in the press; there were no frantic phonecalls from Birmingham. Much to our surprise we'd carried it off. After six months we informed Ireland and Birmingham of my "pregnancy" and put off any visitations with tales of virus problems. Joan's doctor said the birthmark would fade to nothing within a year, even though I was fairly sure that no one present at the birth had noticed it. Jack, as we called him after his surrogate grandad, had no birth certificate, but Joan said she had a contact and we would get one made up for the day of my pretend delivery. He would always be a year ahead of himself.

Jake wrote to me. He knew I had Deirdre's child. He promised to keep the secret unless she showed signs of curiosity, of wanting to find him. Good man. Shortly after that, Deirdre contracted TB and spent a year in a sanatorium. I took Jack to visit her a few times. She was gentle and loving with him. I ached to tell her the truth, but Joan, Jake and me decided it wasn't a good idea. I still don't know if we were right. When she was well Jake took her back home to fresh air, vegetables, gossip and Father Molloy. Mam and Dad were delighted. It shows on the photos Jake sends from time to time. Deirdre has put on weight too; she looks buoyant and beautiful. She's unable to have any more children, but her and Jake have taken to fostering a string of misfits. Who better?

I haven't been home at all since the day my bags were packed for me, but Jack is already asking about visiting his grandparents across the sea. There's a letter, written and waiting for him in Isobel's writing box. He'll get it when he's sixteen. Then, who knows what will happen.

Dan and Louie got married. She's been off the game for some time. The pub continues to be a sanctuary for Irish exiles. Nancy has the makings of an extraordinary musician. She plays with a group of six, all second-generation Irish. They're called the DPs (Displaced Persons).

Breda and Mick just couldn't make their land work for them in any way that made economic sense, so, at long last, she joined me in England. Jack Senior got Mick on at the pit. Breda is pregnant with their third child. Meantime, Bridget Isobel Kelly and her sister, Shelagh, are a great influence on Jack Murphy.

When I met Kevin O'Mara, political agitator, union organiser, friend of Dan Kavanagh, I was impressed. I shook his hand and recalled what Dan had said about there being no confusion when you look love in the eye. He has fire in his guts and the conversation of a poet. He believes it is the curse of the Irish in England to cry for their homeland, to be prepared to die for the homeland when what they need to do is join in the struggles for justice in England. It makes a harsh sort of sense.

God hasn't spoken to me since that runaway night when I stole Deirdre's baby. He must be dead, because He couldn't keep His mouth shut when He was alive.

Acknowledgements

A big thank you for their help during the writing of this book to:
Peter Mortimer for his love and optimism; Jo Williams; Mary
Fitzgerald, my mother; her sisters Kitty, Madge, Josie, Nellie, Bridie, and
all my cousins for being who they are. Sally Walker, Deborah Carey,
Niall Culverwell, Chrissie Glazebrook and Elaine Drainville for their
faith in me. Bernard and Mary Loughlin at the Tyrone Guthrie Centre,
Co. Monaghan, where the first draft was completed; Jenny Attala and
Northern Arts for their encouragement and financial support; Andrea
Badenoch, Julia Darling and Debbie Taylor for their constructive
comments, and keeping me going; Carol Bell and Cumbria County
Council for their support; Jan Maloney, Sarah Davidson, Esther Salamon,
David Stephenson, Barry Stone, Paul Simpson and everyone at Amber
Films for being there; Tom Jennings for his patience, and Steve MacDonogh
for his enthusiasm.

J. M. O'Neill / *Duffy Is Dead*

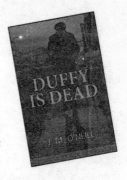

A mournful, funny, warm comedy of
Islington-to-Hackney Irish low-life, lovingly
set among the streets, shops, pubs and people
of London.

"A book written sparingly, with wit and without
sentimentality, yet the effect can be like poetry...
An exceptional novel." *Guardian*

"The atmosphere is indescribable but absolutely right: as if the world of
Samuel Beckett had crossed with that of George V. Higgins." *Observer*

ISBN 0 86322 261 7; paperback £6.99

J. M. O'Neill / *Open Cut*

Hennessy lived in London: grafted, struggled
and eked out his days in a London respectable
people are careful never to see. A construction
site world of 'kerbside sweat, open-cut trenches,
timbered shafts'. A bleak, desolate world of
whisky-dulled pain, casual brutality and corruption.
But Hennessy planned a change to his station in life.
An abrupt and violent change.

"O'Neill's prose, like the winter wind is cutting and sharp."
British Book News

"An uncannily exacting and accomplished novelist." *Observer*

"Exciting and dangerous, with a touch of the poet." *Sunday Times*

ISBN 0 86322 264 1; paperback £6.99

John Trolan / *Slow Punctures*

"Compelling... his writing, with its mix of
brutal social realism, irony and humour, reads like
a cross between Roddy Doyle and Irvine Welsh."
Sunday Independent

"Three hundred manic, readable pages...
Slow Punctures is grim, funny and bawdy in equal
measure." *The Irish Times*

"Fast-moving and hilarious in the tradition of Roddy Doyle."
Sunday Business Post

"Trolan writes in a crisp and consistent style. He handles the delicate
subject of young suicide with a sensitive practicality and complete lack
of sentiment. His novel is a brittle working-class rites of passage that
tells a story about Dublin that probably should have been told a long
time ago." *Irish Post*

ISBN 0 86322 252 8; original paperback £8.99

David Rice / *Song of Tiananmen Square*

"A story of love in the time of trouble: love
between an Irish lecturer Peter John O'Connor
and a beautiful young Chinese student Song Lan...
A racy novel... [and] a worthwhile reminder... that
when the shooting stopped in Tiananmen Square in
1989 the torture did not end." *Sunday Tribune*

"Ten years after the killings in and around Tiananmen, David Rice has
recreated the sights, sounds, smells and above all the emotions of
Beijing in the spring of 1989." Jonathan Mirsky, who reported
Tiananmen for the *Observer*

"Bringing alive the struggle for freedom and human rights, this tale has
at its heart a story of love and friendship pushed to breaking point."
Irish News

ISBN 0 86322 251 X; original paperback £8.99